Careful What You Wish

ASHLEY FARLEY

Copyright © 2022 by Ashley Farley

All rights reserved.

Leisure Time Books, a division of AHF Publishing

All rights reserved. No part of this book may be used or reproduced in any manner without written permission from the author.

This book is a work of fiction. Names, characters, establishments, organizations, and incidents are either products of the author's imagination or are used fictitiously to give a sense of authenticity. Any resemblance to actual persons, living or dead, events, or locales is entirely coincidental.

DEDICATION

For our wonderful readers in My Book Friends

ALSO BY ASHLEY FARLEY

Hope Springs Series
Dream Big, Stella!
Show Me the Way
Mistletoe and Wedding Bells
Matters of the Heart
Road to New Beginnings

Palmetto Island Series
Muddy Bottom
Change of Tides
Lowcountry on My Mind
Sail Away

Stand Alone
Tangled in Ivy
Lies that Bind
Life on Loan
Only One Life
Nell and Lady
Sweet Tea Tuesdays

CHAPTER 1

Mary stands at the second-floor master bedroom window, watching the mistress of the house back out of the driveway and peel off down the road in her white convertible Mercedes. Daisy Crawford attends daily yoga classes and works out three times a week with her personal trainer. She plays tennis at her country club on Mondays and Wednesdays. Attends garden club meetings on Tuesdays. Meets friends for boozy lunches that last well into the afternoons on Fridays. She spends Thursday mornings catching up on work at her desk but reserves Thursday afternoons for beauty appointments— hair and nails, facials and mud wraps. Daisy often complains about her hectic schedule. The pampered woman doesn't know how lucky she's got it.

Daisy is originally from Georgia. She puts on the sugary sweet Southern belle act when she's manipulating others into doing her bidding. But Daisy is far from sweet. Mary has seen her in action many times. She's a vampire out for blood.

That's not to say Mary doesn't admire her employer. She

aspires to be more like her, with oodles of friends and invitations to the best parties in town.

Daisy and Mary are besties when no one else is around. Over coffee in the mornings, Daisy confides in Mary about her problems. The lawn crew, who are always slacking off. Vera at the Curl Up & Dye Salon, who can never get her hair the desired shade of honey blonde. The dry cleaners, who can never get the creases in her husband's pants straight. When Daisy's friends are around, however, she treats Mary like the hired help. Which, of course, she is.

Mary has worked for the Crawfords for nearly ten years. She manages every aspect of Daisy's domestic life. Cleaning and laundry. Grocery shopping and cooking. The Crawfords, including their two teenage daughters, make Mary's job easier by being neat freaks. They make their beds every morning. Never leave dishes in the sink. And always return wet bath towels to the rack for drying. While this isn't her dream job, Mary is grateful for the modest income.

Mary leaves the window and throws open the double doors to Daisy's walk-in closet. The closet is organized according to garment. One wall, divided into two compartments, is designated for hanging garments. Long and short dresses for every occasion occupy one side, while slacks, skirts, and blouses hang from two racks on the other. Shelves housing cashmere sweaters in every color occupy another wall, and on the third, cubbies provide space for shoes, accessories, and a small jewelry safe.

Mary has been eyeing the latest addition to Daisy's extensive collection of haute couture, an elegant evening gown in black and white sequins. Stripping off her uniform, Mary tugs the fine garment over her head and slips her feet into a pair of black satin Jimmy Choo sandals. She punches the code into the safe's keypad and rifles through the velvet jewelry boxes. She clips clusters of diamonds to her earlobes, strings multiple strands of pearls around her neck, and fastens a diamond tennis bracelet to her arm.

Mary waltzes out of the closet and pirouettes around the bedroom, imagining herself at a glamorous ball in the arms of her dashing husband with all her friends admiring her from the edge of the dance floor. The sight of her reflection in the full-length mirror stops her dead in her tracks. She possesses the glamour of a bag lady. Her emerald eyes are in stark contrast to her pale face, and her strawberry-blonde locks are a frizzy mess. Mary imagines the sequined fabric hugging Daisy's curves, a long, tanned leg visible through the thigh-high slit. Mary has a little bosom and a flat butt, so the dress hangs on her thin frame like a potato sack. She's like a child playing dress-up in her mama's clothes. Only Mary isn't a child. She's the pathetic housekeeper coveting her employer's worldly possessions.

The weight of Mary's problems suddenly bears down on her. She's exhausted after staying up half the night fretting over her mounting pile of bills. She takes off the spiked heels, hurling them into the corner, and plods on the lush wool carpet over to the king-size bed. She lowers herself to the edge of the mattress and eyes the fluffy feather pillows. Daisy will be gone for hours, and Mary is caught up on the housework for now. Why not take a little nap before she must start on the Crawfords' dinner? Pulling the covers back, she slips beneath the cool Egyptian linen sheets and closes her eyes.

She's awakened sometime later by the sound of Daisy shrieking. "Mary May! What on earth are you doing in my bed? In my new designer dress?"

Daisy whips back the covers, and with surprising strength, she hauls Mary out of the bed to her feet. "What're you doing wearing my jewelry? You little thief, how did you get into my safe?"

Daisy's blue eyes bulge and her face is as red as a beet. Mary worries her boss's head might explode.

Mary scurries to the closet, but Daisy is on her heels, pawing at her. "Take it off this minute!" She grabs a handful of the sequined dress and yanks hard.

Mary jumps back. "Stop it! Please, Mrs. Crawford! You'll rip the fabric. I know you're upset. But I didn't mean any harm. I just wanted to try on the dress."

"You have exactly one minute to give me back my jewelry." Daisy holds out her hand, collecting the pieces as Mary removes them from her ears, neck, and arm.

Mary stares down at the floor, avoiding Daisy's piercing glare. "May I have some privacy to change?"

"No, you may not! In fact, keep the dress! I don't want it back after it's been on your body. You're fired, Mary." Daisy kicks at Mary's uniform on the floor. "Get your things and go."

Tears sting Mary's eyes. "Please, Mrs. Crawford. If you fire me, I'll lose my house. I know what I did was wrong. And I'm terribly sorry. I'm begging you to give me another chance. I promise, nothing like this will ever happen again."

Daisy's arm shoots out with pearls dangling from her hand as she points at the door. "Get outta my house this instant."

Mary collects her uniform and tennis shoes and escapes the closet. Daisy follows her down the stairs to the laundry room. She removes her lunch box and canvas tote bag from the broom closet and turns to face Daisy. "You'll need to pay me for this week."

Daisy gives her a death stare. "I owe you nothing. You're lucky I don't call the police. You'll never work in this town again."

Stuffing her uniform and shoes in her tote, Mary exits the house through the back door and runs on bare feet down the hot asphalt driveway. When she reaches the sidewalk, she gathers up the bottom of the dress and heads off at a race-walker pace on Main Street.

The town square is a hubbub of activity, with locals and tourists shopping the boutiques and lunching at the many restaurants. People stare at Mary as she makes her way to an empty park bench. It's unusual to see a woman wearing an evening gown in the middle of the day.

A crowd of tourists cluster around the town's famous linden tree, tying their wishes to its branches with satin ribbon. If only these misguided people knew the truth about the tree. That it's a scam.

Linden Falls is a tourist town. Foliage seekers flock here by the thousands every autumn. The chamber of commerce uses the Wishing Tree, the promise of dreams come true, to attract vacationers during the off-season.

Born and raised in Linden Falls, Mary has made her share of wishes over the years. Childish wishes that came true because of her parents, not because of the tree. But the wish that would've changed her life, the one she tied on the tree every single day for over a decade, never came true.

The early June sun is warm on her bare shoulders. Mary closes her eyes and tilts her face to the sky as her new reality hits home. She's really done it this time. She's in a pickle, a red-hot mess. Daisy Crawford will follow through on her threat. Mary will never find another job in Linden Falls. She's been thinking of starting her own business, of marketing her homemade potpourri and herbal teas. She's even purchased the packaging supplies. Even if her business is wildly successful, it won't earn her the money she needs.

If only Mary had completed her education instead of dropping out of high school to marry a deadbeat.

When Mary opens her eyes again, the tourists have moved away from the tree. She puts on her tennis shoes and approaches the tree. She eyes the ribboned wishes as she circles the trunk. She says out loud, "Everyone's ultimate dream is to be rich. If you're so great, Mister Tree, why don't your limbs grow money instead of leaves?"

A gentle breeze rustles the leaves, causing Mary's breath to hitch. She watches and waits for the tree to sprout dollar bills. When nothing happens, she gives the tree a swift kick. "You're a fraud, Mister Tree. Just like me." She turns her back to the tree and walks away.

Leaving the square, she strolls south two blocks to Wisteria Lane. Pausing at the corner, her heart sinks at the sight of her dilapidated house nestled in amongst the other stately homes. Hers is the largest on the street but also the one most in need of repairs. Mary's great-grandfather, one of the town's founding fathers, built the house in the early 1920s. It has remained in their family ever since.

Mary loves the wide porches and spacious rooms. But paint is peeling off the wood siding, and the brick steps are crumbling. Shutters are rotting, and a few of the gutters have fallen off. Six months ago, a *concerned* neighbor wrote her a letter, asking her to either fix up her house or sell it. She currently has five hundred dollars in her bank account, and she'll never see the money Orville, her ex-husband, owes her in alimony. Now that she's lost her job, she'll have no choice but to sell. In its current state, she'll be hard-pressed to get market value. But there's good news. With no mortgage, whatever sum she gets from the buyer will be money in her pocket.

Two children—a boy and girl who look enough alike to be siblings—walk past Mary. The little boy sticks his tongue out at her. "You're that grumpy old lady who lives in the haunted house. My mama says you're a witch."

His sister punches him in the arm. "Shut up, Tommy!

CAREFUL WHAT YOU WISH

That's not nice." Taking him by the hand, she drags him off, tossing an apology over her shoulder at Mary.

Mary cringes. At forty-five, she doesn't consider herself old. Do her neighbors really think of her as a grumpy witch?

She continues toward home. Maybe she'll leave town and start over somewhere new. There's little keeping her in Linden Falls. Only a few wonderful memories sprinkled in with a lot of bad ones. But where would she go? Linden Falls is the only town in the only state she's ever known.

Biscuit greets Mary at the door. He cocks his head to the side, giving her a quizzical look. She massages his ears. "I know, buddy. I'm overdressed for gardening. Let me run upstairs and change."

Her rescue mutt lives for the hours they spend together every afternoon in the backyard. Mary took up gardening years ago, when her friends had babies and she could not conceive. She finds gardening therapeutic. Over time, her flowers have become her friends.

She quickly changes into cutoff jeans and an old T-shirt. Daisy's dress looks out of place hanging alongside Mary's outdated wardrobe in her closet. Mary has no use for the dress. No fancy party to wear it to. Perhaps she'll sell it on eBay. She might get a decent price, enough to pay for gutter repair.

Downstairs in the kitchen, she pauses at the sink for a drink of water. The sunny room lifts her spirits with its oversized windows, old pine farm table, and comfy armchairs where her grandmother used to knit baby blankets. One chair has a broken leg. Mary has glued it back together many times, but she can't bring herself to throw them away.

Biscuit waits with tail wagging beside the back door. When she lets him out, he bolts across the porch, through the screen door, and into the yard. Stuffing her feet into her garden clogs, Mary grabs her sunhat from the coatrack and follows him outside. Years ago, when Mary was a little girl, her father installed a seven-foot privacy fence to protect their family from the prying eyes of their nosey next-door neighbor Beatrice Beckham. Many neighbors have come and gone since Beatrice died, yet the fence remains, a cocoon sheltering her from the outside world.

Mary marvels at her garden in full bloom. Grass covers about an eighth of her yard. The rest is planted with annuals and perennials and flowering shrubs. She has several rare varieties of cultivars, but her old-fashioned tea roses are her favorites. She drops to her knees beside her roses. She's gathering up rose petals to make potpourri when a hundred-dollar bill floats to the ground in front of her. Looking up, she's stunned to see the branches of her old maple tree are covered in crisp paper money.

"Well, I'll be darned. The Wishing Tree creates miracles after all." She claps her hands, and paper currency rains down from the tree, accumulating around her. Cackling like a madwoman, she falls backward into the pile of cash. Biscuit pounces on her, and they roll around in the paper money, laughing and barking until their energy is spent.

"Come on, boy," Mary says, scrambling to her feet. "We need to get this money up before anyone sees it."

Mary spends an hour raking the money onto an old bedsheet and bringing it inside to the kitchen. Seated at the farm table, she separates the bills by denomination into stacks of twenty. She rolls the stacks into bundles, secures the bundles with rubber bands, and places them in an old pillowcase, which she drops into a hidey-hole under the loose floorboard in the walk-in pantry.

She brews a cup of homemade rosehip and hibiscus tea and takes it out to the porch. She stares up at the maple tree, whose leaves are once again green. She counted over ten thousand dollars. Enough to get started on repairs. If only she had a little more money. Would it be greedy to ask for the rest of the money needed to put the house on the market? Perhaps she'll pay another visit to the Wishing Tree tomorrow.

CHAPTER 2

A second visit to the town's Wishing Tree isn't necessary. Mary wakes the following morning to find her backyard covered in paper currency. This time, after she rakes and bundles, she counts nearly twenty thousand dollars.

She spends the afternoon meeting with brick masons, carpenters, and gutter repairmen. When she suggest paying in cash, the contractors offer her a considerable discount and agree to start on the project right away.

When the maple yields another thirty thousand dollars the next morning, she calls the most reputable painting company in town. The estimator informs her the siding must be scraped and primed before it can be repainted. The bid is astronomical, but she'll get it back in the proceeds from the sale of the house.

Every morning, Mary rises before dawn to collect and count the day's bounty before the workmen arrive around seven thirty. She logs the sums into a ledger. The amounts vary, averaging about ten thousand a day. When the hidey-

CAREFUL WHAT YOU WISH

hole in her pantry is full, after dark one evening, she digs a gigantic hole and buries a galvanized trash can in the backyard, using a potted geranium as a lid. She stores her cash bundles in Ziplock bags inside the trash can.

At the end of the first week, when she pays the carpenter for replacing the rotten shutters, he says, "What're you doing with all this cash, lady? Shouldn't you put it in the bank?"

Mary envisions herself wheelbarrowing her daily cash collection to the bank. How would she explain hundreds of thousands of dollars growing on trees? The teller would think she'd lost her mind.

She doesn't like to lie, but in this case, a fib is better than the truth. "My aunt died recently. Since I'm her only living relative, she left me her nest egg, a stash of cash she kept hidden under her mattress. If I put it in the bank, the IRS will come after me."

"You're one lucky lady. Wish I had me a rich dead aunt."

"Maybe you should tie that wish to the Wishing Tree," Mary suggests.

"Nah. I don't believe in miracles," he says and saunters off down the sidewalk to his truck.

Neither did I until last week, she thinks as she watches him go.

Mary rides herd on the workmen. They make mistakes when she's not keeping a close eye on their progress. To compensate for being so demanding, she makes them homemade blueberry muffins in the mornings and serves them sweet peach tea and oatmeal cookies in the afternoons. But having them around is a nuisance. They peek in her windows, pee in her shrubs, and feed Biscuit the leftovers from their lunches. And she's relieved when their work ends the last full week of June.

On Friday afternoon, after all the workmen have gone,

Mary stands in her front yard admiring the improvements. The house is as good as new on the outside. Whoever buys it can deal with the interior renovations.

Sitting down on the porch steps, Mary pulls Biscuit close and strokes his fur while she contemplates her future. What now? She has the money to do anything she wants. She could travel to Paris or Australia. Move to Florida or Colorado. She could go back to school and get her college degree. Or she could stay right here in Linden Falls. She doesn't have to sell now that she has a steady income from the tree.

Mary asks herself what she truly wants out of life. Her answer surprises her. She wants a friend.

Mary has given little thought to finding romance again. In her experience, men aren't worth the time and effort. But she's starved for female companionship. Years ago, she had a falling-out with her childhood besties—Evie and Bess. After she divorced Orville, their couple friends took his side. She even misses her morning talks with Daisy. A thought occurs to Mary. Maybe now that she has money, Daisy will welcome her into her fold.

On Tuesday of the following week, Mary dons her best sundress and sets out on foot to the Bistro Claudine—one of the popular lunch spots Daisy and her friends frequent. The hostess seats her at a table beside two of Daisy's closest friends. Susan Wilbanks is a striking beauty with eyes as dark as the evil that lies within. Jodi Snyder is softer and prettier with chestnut hair and kind brown eyes. When Mary worked for Daisy, Jodi always went out of her way to speak to her.

Mary is sitting facing the window with the women to her left. She senses their eyes on her, and when they talk about her, they don't lower their voices.

"The woman next to us looks familiar," Susan says. "Who is she?"

"You know who that is, Susan. That's Daisy's housekeeper, Mary."

"Oh, right. The one she fired a few weeks ago." Susan takes a closer look. "I should've recognized the scowl. You should give her the name of your Botox provider."

Jodi glares back at Susan. "I don't do Botox."

"Liar. Everyone does Botox." Susan stares back at Mary. "I doubt it would help, anyway. Those frown lines are permanently etched in her forehead."

"Why did Daisy fire her?"

Susan leans toward Jodi. "Haven't you heard? Everyone in town is talking about it. Daisy came home from playing tennis to find Mary sleeping in her bed. She was wearing Daisy's new sequined gown, the one she bought to wear to your formal anniversary party. And get this. Mary also had on some jewelry she took from Daisy's safe."

Jodi gasps. "She broke into her safe? That's awful." Her gaze drifts to Mary, giving her the once-over. "Poor thing. Look at that sundress she's wearing. She just wanted to know what it was like to wear nice clothes."

Susan snickers. "You're probably right. That sundress is vintage Walmart, circa the turn of the century."

Mary's throat swells as she pushes back from the table. Grabbing her purse, she hurries to the women's restroom, locking the door behind her. She leans against the door, gulping in air until her breath steadies. She splashes cold water on her face and dries it with a brown paper towel. Susan's words come back to her as she studies her frown lines in the mirror. *I should've recognized the scowl.* When is the last time Mary smiled? The last time she had anything to smile about? Before Orville cheated on her and left her for his pregnant mistress. Before her fertility specialist informed her there was no hope.

Tommy, her little neighbor, called her a grumpy old lady.

Is that why she has no friends? Because she's forgotten how to smile?

Mary refuses to stick needles in her face no matter how much money the tree drops. But she can concentrate on being more pleasant to others. And she can do something about her wardrobe. Mary looks down at her floral sundress. She bought it to wear when she eloped with Orville. Way before the turn of the century.

Mary leaves the restroom and exits the restaurant. She enters Caroline's, the women's fashion boutique next door. Two salesclerks, a redhead and a blonde, are dressing a mannequin at the back of the store. When they see Mary, their smiles fade. The redhead calls out, "Can I help you with something?"

Mary yells back, "I'm just looking. If that's okay."

"Of course," the redhead says. "Make yourself at home."

Mary flips through the racks of clothing, draping the items she'd like to try on over one arm. She's soon loaded down with short, flouncy dresses, designer jeans, and dressy tops. She's always dreamed of having designer clothes like Daisy's. The women of this town will notice her now, when she strolls down Main Street in her new wardrobe.

The blonde clerk finally relieves her of the clothes. "Here, let me put those in a dressing room for you."

"Thanks." Mary grabs a few more items and goes into the fitting room.

The salesclerks are right outside the door, adding accessories to the mannequin, and Mary can hear them whispering as she tries on a pair of gray linen slacks and a white sleeveless top.

"Is she a tourist? I've never seen her before."

"I have no idea. But did you see her dress? I doubt she can afford to shop here."

"Watch her closely. Make sure she doesn't shoplift."

Mary gathers up all the clothes, including her outdated sundress, and marches out of the dressing room in the outfit she was trying on. She plunks everything down on the checkout counter. "I'll take it all," she says to the salesclerks. "And I'll pay in cash."

"Cash?" the redhead asks.

"Cash," she repeats, removing a bundle of hundreds from her purse.

The redhead tallies up her charges while the blonde folds and bags the clothing. The total is just over two thousand dollars. Mary peels off twenty-one from her bundle and hands it to the redhead.

Mary takes her purchases and sashays out of the boutique. She's walking home on Main Street when a bright blue flier stapled to a telephone pole catches her attention. She pauses to read the invitation to the annual Fourth of July parade and picnic in the town square. She hasn't attended the event in years. But she should go. She might run into old friends or make new ones. It's important she looks her best. She still has work to do to prepare.

She rips the flier from the pole, folds it into her purse, and hurries home. After neatly hanging her new wardrobe in her closet, she schedules a hair and nail appointment for Friday at the Curl Up & Dye salon. Opening her ancient laptop, she spends the afternoon shopping online for clothes, shoes, and accessories. She expedites shipping and charges everything to her credit card. She'll figure out a way to use her cash when the bills roll in.

MARY ARRIVES EARLY on Friday for her appointment at the beauty salon. The nail technician greets her at the door. "Don't worry, hon. I had a cancellation. I can take you now."

Mary has never had a professional mani and pedi, and she relishes being pampered. She chooses a hot pink polish for her toes and a sheer pale pink for her fingers. When her nails are done, the technician shows Mary to the stylist's station. "Vera will be right with you," she says and scurries away.

While she waits, Mary thumbs through the latest issue of *Better Homes and Gardens* magazine. She eavesdrops on snippets of conversation around her. Everyone is getting pretty for the big Fourth of July picnic. Some are planning elaborate feasts under rented tents in the square. One woman's daughter, the head of the high school cheerleading squad, will lead the parade.

A young apprentice appears in the mirror behind Mary. She drapes a cape around her, fastening it at the back of her neck, and walks her to the shampoo bowl for washing and conditioning. Vera is waiting for her when she returns to the station.

The stylist, with her curvaceous figure and bleached hair piled on top of her head, is a legend in this town. She talks like a sailor and drinks like a fish, but she's a magician at styling hair.

"You have a lovely head of hair, a true strawberry-blonde." Vera combs through her damp locks. "I don't see a single strand of gray. But your ends are damaged. How long has it been since you had it cut?"

"I can't remember. It's been years. I was thinking about a style similar to this." Mary shows Vera a photo in the *Better Homes* magazine of a woman with shoulder-length, layered hair.

Vera scoops up her hair, holding it so it grazes her shoulders. "That would be lovely. But, in order to achieve the look, we'll have to cut off at least four inches."

"I can live with that," Mary says. "As long as I can still pull it back in a ponytail."

"Of course." Vera clips the top layers of hair on top of Mary's head and begins shearing inches off the bottom layer. "I don't think I've seen you before. Are you from around these parts?"

"I've lived here all my life, actually."

Vera removes a slip of paper from her apron pocket. "Mary May. Is that a double name or first and last?"

"First and last. I'm Mary Ellis May. Although I'm no longer married to Mr. May."

Vera returns the paper to her pocket. "The name rings a bell. By any chance, did you used to work for Daisy Crawford?"

Mary grimaces. "Guilty as charged."

Vera locks eyes with Mary in the mirror. "Daisy told me about finding you dressed in her evening attire and sleeping in her bed. Is it true?"

A hush descends over the salon as the other patrons and stylists wait for Mary's reaction. "It was an unfortunate mistake. One I prefer to forget."

"You have nothing to be embarrassed about, Mary May. It's the funniest story I've heard in this salon in all the years I've been working here. Daisy is running her mouth all over town about you. Everyone thinks it's absolutely hilarious."

"Great, so now I'm the laughingstock of the town," Mary mumbles, sinking down in the chair.

Mary tunes Vera out as she chatters on about Daisy's uppity ways. She doesn't care for gossip and feels almost sorry for Daisy. Vera snips away at her hair, and Mary is thrilled with the outcome. The layers framing her face make her appear ten years younger.

Vera walks Mary to the checkout counter, eyeing her suspiciously when she removes a wad of cash from her wallet. But when Mary gives her a generous tip, Vera grins and says, "Come back soon, now, ya hear?"

It appears Mary has made one friend in this town.

CHAPTER 3

Mary thinks of the Fourth of July picnic as her coming out party, and she spends the weekend preparing for the big event on Sunday. To preserve her manicure, she's careful to wear her garden gloves when working in the yard. Her online orders arrive, and she tries on several outfits before deciding on white designer skinny jeans and a patriotic blouse—stars on one side and stripes on the other with bell sleeves and shoulders cut out. Her cheeks tire from smiling at herself in the mirror, and she nearly sprains her ankle while practicing walking in her peek-toe wedges.

The Fourth dawns bright with cloudless skies and moderate temperatures. Mary can hardly contain her excitement as she completes her chores. She takes a long, hot shower and extra care in styling her hair and putting on makeup. When four o'clock finally arrives, she migrates with the rest of the townsfolk to Main Street for the parade. She purchases an American stick flag from a teenager and positions herself at the sidewalk's edge for an unobstructed view of the procession of antique cars and area high school marching bands.

The crowd follows the parade to the square, where food trucks are waiting to serve hot dogs, hamburgers, and pulled-pork barbecue. A stage, draped in patriotic bunting, is positioned in one corner of the square in anticipation of the entertainment lineup expected later in the evening.

Daisy's tent, by far the largest, occupies the center of the square. Potted geraniums grace banquet tables adorned with red-and-white-checked linens. Servers, clad in black and white, hustle about, preparing a barbecue buffet and offering guests hors d'oeuvres. Daisy is a golden goddess in a slim-fitting sleeveless white dress that shows off her toned and tanned arms and legs. The invitation flier specifically stated no alcohol, but Mary is certain the pale green liquid in her Tervis Tumbler is Daisy's favorite—Skinnygirl Margarita.

Mary approaches Daisy with caution. "Your tent is amazing. Do you have a large crowd joining you for dinner?"

Daisy rolls her eyes, as though speaking to Mary is beneath her. "Just the usual crowd. What do you want, Mary? If you're hoping to get your job back, you can forget it. I've already hired someone new."

The rehearsed lines flow from Mary's lips. "Actually, I don't need to work anymore. My aunt left me some money. A lot of money, in fact."

As Mary suspected, the mention of money gets Daisy's attention. "I don't remember you ever mentioning an aunt."

Mary flicks her layered hair off her shoulders. "I never met her. She lived out west. She apparently never had children of her own. Since I'm her only surviving family, she left her fortune to me."

Daisy crosses her arms over her chest, her Tervis Tumbler dangling from fingertips. "I don't believe you."

Mary shrugs nonchalantly. "It's true."

Irritation creeps across Daisy's expression. "Well, goody for you. Now, run along." She shoos Mary away. "My guests will be here soon."

Mary strolls off. She'll wait until Daisy's margarita buzz kicks in before trying again.

She stands in a long line for a shriveled-up hot dog and bag of chips and wanders around the square looking for somewhere to sit. Panic grips her. She recognizes plenty of people, but no one invites her to join them. She breathes a sigh of relief when she spots Evie and Bess. She drops to her knees onto their picnic blanket. "Mind if I join you?"

Bess and Evie exchange a look. They don't want her either.

"You can stay for a minute," Bess says.

"Our dinner should be ready soon. Our husbands are cooking burgers on the grill." Evie inclines her head at two men standing beside a grill in the shade of a large elm tree. Mary hasn't seen their husbands in so long, she wouldn't have recognized them. Gilbert and Wendell have put on weight and lost most of the hair on top of their heads.

Mary's mouth waters at the thought of juicy hamburgers sizzling on the grill. She looks down at the unappetizing hot dog. Maybe she should trash it and get in line for a hamburger.

Evie follows Mary's gaze to her plate. "That looks disgusting."

"I agree." Mary sets her untouched plate on the blanket. "Are your children here?"

"They're running around here somewhere." Bess studies Mary closely. "Why are you grinning like that? Is something wrong with your lips?"

Mary presses her lips wider. "What do you mean? I'm smiling because I'm happy. It's the Fourth of July."

"Why are you here, Mary?" Evie asks in a deadpan tone.

Mary looks back and forth between her old friends. Neither has changed much, aside from a few lines around their eyes and pounds around their waists. "That's an odd question. I'm here for the same reason as you, the parade and picnic."

Evie jabs the blanket with her finger. "I mean here, here. With us."

Mary lets out an awkward laugh. "I haven't seen you in a while, and I thought it'd be fun to catch up."

Evie scoffs. "We'd been friends since childhood, and out of the blue, for no apparent reason, you ditched us. And now you want to catch up?"

"I'm not buying it either," Bess adds. "Whenever we see you in public, you run the other way. Then you plop down here like nothing ever happened. You can't blame us for being suspicious."

Evie looks pointedly at her. "You owe us an explanation, Mary."

Mary squirms and looks away. The moment of truth has come. Perhaps if she'd explained her feelings back then, they could've remained friends. "That was a tough time for me. I was trying so hard to conceive, and the two of you were having babies one after another. It hurt too much to be around you."

Bess says, "So instead of being happy for us, you became resentful. And that resentfulness turned into bitterness."

"Something like that," Mary says. "You had to be in my shoes to understand what I was going through."

A pack of preteens with pimply faces and crooked teeth plops down on the blanket. The children stare at Mary, as though curious about the stranger who has crashed their picnic, but neither Bess nor Evie introduce Mary.

When one girl asks Bess for money for ice cream, Mary slips away. She dumps her plate in a nearby trash can and wanders about aimlessly, unsure of what to do with herself. The thought of going home to an empty house depresses her. She had such high hopes for the picnic, her coming out party. How is it possible to be surrounded by hundreds of people and still feel so all alone?

When a small bluegrass band begins to play on stage, Mary makes her way to the edge of the dance floor, standing at an unoccupied bar-height table. Here, with people dancing and cheering on the band, no one notices she's by herself. The music boosts her spirits, and she stays through the next several groups—a wedding singer, an a cappella quartet, and a gospel singer who brings down the house. The sun begins its descent, and the crowd gets a little rowdy. Mary is making her way to the drinks table for some sweet tea when she collides with Daisy. The red liquid in Daisy's tumbler splashes down the front of her white dress, and she lets out a squeal that gets everyone's attention.

"Look what you've done!" Daisy shrieks.

Mary grabs some napkins and rubs at the stain. "I'm pretty sure you stumbled into me. But it doesn't matter. I'm sorry it happened."

Daisy brushes Mary's hand away. "Stop touching me. Susan! Jodi! Get over here right now." In a blink of an eye, Daisy's friends are at her side.

"What happened?" Susan says, pressing her fingers to her lips to hide her smile.

Daisy sweeps an arm at Mary. "This nitwit ran into me."

Jodi gives Mary an apologetic glance. "I'm not so sure about that, Daisy. I was watching. I think maybe you ran into her."

Anger flashes in Daisy's eyes. "You don't know what you're talking about. Go to my house and get me a change of clothes," she demands of Jodi. "Bring me my white jeans and my blue sleeveless silk top. The one I wore to your party last month."

"Why don't you come with me," Jodi suggests. "A break from the party and a cup of coffee might do you good."

Through gritted teeth, Daisy says, "I don't need coffee." She spins Jodi around and plants her foot in Jodi's behind. "Go!"

Jodi slinks off with head lowered.

Daisy glares at Mary. "What're you looking at? You caused this mess."

"Jodi saw the whole thing. This is *your* fault, not mine. I hope your new housekeeper can get the stain out." Mary brushes past Daisy, and holding her head high, she crosses Main Street toward Wisteria Lane.

She replays the scene in her mind on the way home. Daisy is a bigger monster than Mary realized. Who does she think she is, ordering Jodi around like that? And why does Jodi take it? Mary would rather not have any friends than friends like Daisy.

CHAPTER 4

Mary wakes on July fifth with a bee in her bonnet to buy a car. After raking and counting the day's supply of Maple Money, she takes a taxi to the used car lot on the outskirts of town. She hasn't driven a car in years, and she's not sure she remembers how. A middle-aged man with a bad comb-over and a turkey neck comes out to greet her. "Hey there, little lady. Looking to buy a car today?"

"That's the idea. I'm looking for something flashy," she says with Daisy's Mercedes convertible in mind.

"You're in luck. I have several excellent choices on the lot right now. Come with me." He waves her on, and she crosses the parking lot behind him. She walks down the row of luxury sedans and SUVs, peeking through the windows at the interiors and studying sticker costs. She gawks when she sees the cost of a silver Range Rover. "Isn't that a lot for a ten-year-old car?"

The salesman chuckles. "Not for a Range Rover. You're paying for the brand. I can put you in a newer model Tahoe for a lot less money and mileage."

She catches sight of a small slate-blue pickup truck. She envisions herself driving home from the garden center with the truck's bed overflowing with plants and Biscuit riding in the passenger seat with his head hanging out the window. But a pickup truck won't present the image she's hoping for.

"What's the best deal you can give me on the Range Rover if I pay cash?"

His forehead lines deepen. "Cash?" he asks, and she holds up a pillowcase filled with bundles of hundreds. "Cash."

He massages the flabby skin under his chin. "I been selling cars all my adult life. I ain't never had anyone pay cash for one before."

Mary bops him on the arm with her pillowcase. "There's a first time for everything."

"Don't you wanna test drive it before you buy it?"

Mary is afraid she might make a fool out of herself. Or even worse, she might wreck. "That's not necessary."

The salesman looks at her as if she's lost her mind, but he doesn't argue. "Give me a minute." He disappears inside and returns with a number written on a slip of paper. "This is the best we can do."

The price is only slightly reduced. "Hmm. I don't know." She circles the Range Rover again, but her gaze keeps drifting to the pickup truck. "This is a lot of car for me. What if I decide I don't like it? Do you offer a money-back guarantee?"

"That's why we encourage our customers to test-drive." He flashes her a grin, but when she doesn't smile back, he adds, "But we want you to be satisfied. If the Range Rover isn't right, we'll find something that is."

Mary perks up, her chin high. "In that case, I'll take it."

All eyes are on Mary when she enters the dealership to conduct her transaction. Everyone wants a peek at the woman paying cash for a Range Rover.

Ninety minutes later, Mary pulls slowly off the car lot in her new-to-her Range Rover. She drives the country roads outside of Linden Falls, brushing up on her driving skills and familiarizing herself with the car. When she feels more confident with the car, she returns to town. She rolls down her window, and like a beauty queen in a parade, she drives down Main Street and around the square, smiling and waving at pedestrians. No one pays her any attention.

Mary is making her way toward home when she spots Jodi headed in the opposite direction in a beat-up minivan. Mary makes a sudden U-turn and follows Jodi to a street with small cookie-cutter houses in a less desirable part of town.

Jodi pulls into the driveway of a cheerful yellow house with dormer windows and an inviting front porch. Mary is confused. Is this where Jodi lives? Doesn't she own a big, fancy house like Daisy's?

Pulling to the curb, Mary watches Jodi unload several bags of groceries from the backseat and carry them inside. Mary looks around at the other homes on Cherry Street. Lawns are well-tended and planters overflow with bright flowers. Bench swings and rocking chairs occupy front porches. Children are playing in sprinklers and riding bicycles on the sidewalks. The houses might not be the biggest or prettiest in town, but the street has an upbeat vibe, as though the people who live here are happy.

MARY SPENDS the next several days following Jodi around town. Besides her frequent trips to the country club, Jodi visits Linden Falls Fitness every morning for sweaty workouts. She chauffeurs her teenage daughter to and from a part-time job at Doc's Fountain, an establishment in Linden

Falls known for its old-fashioned sodas but offering trendy coffee drinks as well. Jodi goes for a blowout at the Curl Up & Dye on Wednesday and to the dentist on Thursday morning. Jodi doesn't seem like the gardening type, and Mary finds it fascinating when Jodi spends an entire afternoon wandering around the lawn and garden section at Duncan's Hardware. Jodi frequents the same places as Daisy, is friends with the same group of women, yet something is different about her.

When Jodi's husband arrives home from work in a white truck bearing the Crawford Custom Home Builders logo, Mary connects the dots. Jodi's husband works for Daisy's husband. He is likely a project manager. Which explains why they live in a modest home on Cherry Street. And why Jodi is always at Daisy's beck and call. For Jodi's husband to keep his job, Jodi must do everything Daisy says.

Late in the morning on Saturday, Mary follows Jodi to the country club for lunch with friends on the terrace. Mary wonders how a project manager for a residential builder can afford a membership at a country club. Either the membership is a job perk or Jodi is here as Daisy's guest. Either arrangement deepens Jodi's obligation to Daisy.

The air is muggy, and Mary leaves the engine running with the air conditioning blasting while she waits. She closes her eyes for a minute. Next thing she knows, Jodi is tapping on her window.

Mary rolls the window down. "Can I help you?" she asks with a hint of irritation that suggests Jodi is disturbing her.

Jodi peers at her over the top of her designer sunglass frames. "Are you following me?"

"I . . . um . . ." Mary spots a group of teenagers with tennis racquets. "I came to pick up my friend's kid from tennis practice. Why would you think I'm following you?"

"I just . . . Never mind." Jodi steps away from the car. "I

thought I'd seen your car parked on my street this week. I guess I was mistaken."

"No worries," Mary says and rolls her window back up.

She waits for Jodi to leave before driving home. She'll have to stop following her. Now that Jodi is on to her, she'll be on the lookout for her. Anyway, Mary's mission is complete. Now she knows why Jodi, who is different from Daisy's other friends, is allowed to be part of their group.

MARY RARELY DRINKS COFFEE, but on Sunday morning, after her money chores are complete, she gets a strong hankering for a latte. She strolls over to the square, and she's sipping her drink at an outside table at the Crooked Porch when Jodi emerges from inside with coffee in hand. Jodi looks around, as though searching for somewhere to sit, but all the tables are full. When Jodi spots her, Mary gives her a shy smile and waves her over.

"Are you following me now?" Mary asks, and they both laugh.

Mary gestures at the empty chair opposite her. "Care to join me?"

Jodi casts a nervous glance at the door before taking a seat. "Okay. But only for a minute. I'm meeting friends." She hangs her bag on the back of the chair and crosses her legs. "I've never seen you in here before."

"I'm more of a tea person."

"I drink a lot of tea as well, hot and iced." Jodi eyes Mary's chipped and dirty fingernails. "Are you a gardener?"

"I am. Are you?" Mary asks, even though she already knows the answer.

Jodi nods. "I find yard work therapeutic."

Mary's gaze shifts to Jodi's hands. Her nails are perfectly

shaped and painted a pale pink, much like the color Mary chose for her Fourth of July manicure. "You do a much better job of taking care of your nails than me."

"That's because I don't get as much time to work in the yard as I'd like." Jodi tells Mary about the dahlias she's currently nursing, which leads to a discussion about lilies and hydrangeas. They're so engrossed in their discussion, neither notices Daisy approach until she's looming over their table.

"What on earth are you doing with *her*?" Daisy throws a nod in Mary's direction while her steely glare remains on Jodi.

Jodi jumps to her feet. "I was waiting for you. There was nowhere else to sit."

Daisy looks around the porch, and seeing that all the tables are occupied, she says to Jodi, "You should've waited inside."

Mary smiles at Daisy. "You're welcome to join us. I'm sure we can find another chair."

Daisy lets out a humph, as though offended Mary would dare suggest such a thing. She grabs hold of Jodi's arm. "Come on. We'll go to Doc's Fountain."

"But I already have a drink," Jodi says.

"Get rid of it," Daisy snaps. "You can buy another one at Doc's."

As Daisy leads her away, Jodi casts an apologetic look over her shoulder at Mary.

Mary waits until Jodi and Daisy exit the porch before abandoning her table. She thinks a lot about friendship as she wanders around the square, finishing her latte. Do all friendships come with strings attached? Everyone must benefit from the relationship, otherwise the relationship has no purpose? Jodi does what Daisy wants in exchange for Jodi's husband keeping his job. Bess and Evie blame Mary for dropping them as friends. But, in reality, they ran Mary off. Mary could not have children. Which meant she had nothing to contribute to their conversations. Which meant she no longer belonged in their club.

By the time Mary reaches her street, she concludes genuine friendships based on common interests and mutual respect are rare.

There's not a soul in sight as she walks down the sidewalk. She takes note of the houses on Wisteria Lane, so dignified and pristine with lush green lawns. But they are also so cold and uninviting. None of the residences welcome guests with bright flowers or comfortable seating. Things were different when Mary was growing up here. Children played together, and adults stopped one another in the street to chat. Her mama brought homemade chicken noodle soup to sick neighbors and casseroles when loved ones passed away. That special neighborly camaraderie is still happening on Jodi's street. Why can't it happen on hers?

Mary loads Biscuit in the car, and they drive to Duncan's Hardware, where she purchases a wooden bench swing, four rocking chairs, two ceiling fans, a handful of hanging ferns, and four ceramic planters spilling purple petunias. She arranges for the rockers, fans, and swing to be delivered and loads the rest in her car.

Her delivery arrives first thing on Monday morning, and that afternoon, her carpenter installs the overhead fans. And that evening, Mary makes herself comfortable in one of her new rockers with a glass of ice-cold lemonade. With Biscuit on the floor beside her, she calls out to the neighbors with warm greetings as they pass by. When they don't respond, she doesn't let it get to her. She has faith they'll eventually come around.

CHAPTER 5

Mary is in the kitchen mixing up a batch of lavender potpourri on Wednesday afternoon when her doorbell rings. Unaccustomed to visitors, she cracks open the front door and peeks out. Her heart skips a beat at the sight of a police officer standing on her front porch.

Mary opens the door wider and steps out onto the porch. "May I help you?" she asks, looking up at the imposing figure.

He consults a notepad in his hand. "Are you Mary Ellis May?"

Mary holds her head high. "I am. And you are?"

"Hector Norton, the police chief. I'm here to investigate an accusation made by your ex-employer. Daisy Crawford claims you stole cash from her jewelry safe."

Mary blurts, "She's lying. I never saw any cash in her safe." She realizes her mistake too late.

The chief's dark beady eyes narrow. "So, you admit to breaking into her safe?"

"I . . . um . . . I didn't break into her safe. I had the combination. I didn't mean any harm. I just wanted to try on her jewelry."

The chief flips his notepad to a clean page. "And where did you get the combination?" he asks, his pen poised to jot down her answer.

"Mrs. Crawford can never remember numbers and passwords, so she keeps a list in the back of her address book. She often asked me to look something up for her."

He scrawls something on his notepad. "I have a warrant to search the place."

"But you can't do that. You need probable cause." Mary knows this from watching too many episodes of *CSI*.

He waves a folded sheet of paper. "I have the warrant signed by the judge. I rarely get involved in cases on this level, but Bob Crawford is an important man in this town."

Mary steps in front of the door. "I need to consult with my lawyer before I let you in."

"Do you have a lawyer?"

"No, but—"

"That's what I thought." He nudges her out of the way. "You have nothing to worry about. Unless, of course, you're hiding something."

Mary gulps back fear. She's hiding plenty. Hundreds of thousands of dollars in cash. But it has nothing to do with Daisy Crawford.

The chief orders Mary to wait on the porch. He motions to two uniformed officers in a patrol car at the curb, and the threesome disappears inside.

Mary paces back and forth on the porch with Biscuit nipping at her heels. She's not worried about her hidey-hole in the pantry or the buried trash can in the backyard. Her primary concern is her most recent hiding place—an old steamer trunk in the attic. Did she remember to lock it back after dumping in the morning's stash of cash? What will she do if the police find it? If she uses the dead aunt lie, Chief Norton will insist on verifying her story. There's no way to trace the cash, no way to verify whether she stole the money from Daisy. But she looks guilty. An innocent person would put cash in the bank, not hide it in the attic. Maybe she should tell the truth. Honesty is usually the best policy.

The chief emerges from the house an hour later with several bundles of cash. "Care to explain this? We found it and a bunch more in the attic."

Mary lets out a sigh. "I made a wish on the Wishing Tree in the square. Well, sort of. It wasn't exactly a wish. More of a dare. I asked the tree why its limbs didn't grow money. And I called it a fraud. Next thing I know, the maple in my backyard is sprouting twenty-, fifty-, and hundred-dollar bills."

The chief's bushy brow hits his hairline. "You expect me to believe that cockamamie story?"

Mary plants a hand on her hip. "I realize it sounds farfetched. But stranger wishes have been granted by the tree."

The chief lets out a grunt. "Show me this *magical* maple tree."

Mary leads him through the house. She's relieved to see they didn't ransack her home during their search. They cross the screened porch and step out into the yard. She gestures at the tree. "There she is, Miss Money Maple."

He shields his eyes from the sun as he looks more closely at the tree. "I don't see any money."

"Because the tree sheds it during the night. I rake up the cash before dawn every morning."

Chief Norton tosses his hands in the air. "This is nonsense. Just plain hogwash."

Mary shrugs. "I guess you'll have to come back tomorrow to see for yourself."

He gives her a curt nod. "I guess I will. I'll be here in the morning at five."

When he starts off around the side of the house, Mary calls after him, "Can we keep this between us for now?"

Over his shoulder, he hollers back, "If word leaks out, it didn't come from my office."

But when Mary retrieves her *Linden Falls Gazette* from the front porch the following morning, she's stunned to see a photograph of her house featured on the front page with a headline that reads, "Miss Money Maple."

She skims the article. The reporter makes her out to be a lunatic. While her name isn't disclosed, the story features a picture of her house and mentions Wisteria Lane. She's still staring at the paper when the chief arrives five minutes later.

Mary waves the paper in his face. "Care to explain this? I specifically asked you not to leak this story."

He jabs his finger at the paper. "That didn't come from my office."

"Oh, yeah? Then how did the paper hear about it?" She smacks the newspaper against his chest. "Only four people know about the tree. You, me, and your two officers."

"The media works in mysterious ways, Ms. May. When the police get involved in a case, the press has the uncanny ability of finding out about it. Now, show me the tree. I wanna see your miracle money."

"Fine." She stomps off the porch with the chief trailing behind her.

At the side of the house, she opens the gate and steps aside for him to enter the backyard ahead of her. They round the back corner of the house together, and Mary stops dead in her tracks at the sight of the bare grass. For the first time since making the wish, the tree grew no cash.

The chief looks from the tree to Mary. "Did you collect the money already?"

"No. I haven't been out here this morning. I don't understand it."

"I understand it perfectly. You're trying to pull a fast one on me, Ms. May. You fabricated your little lie to cover for your theft. Just like you told Daisy Crawford that your aunt died and left you a fortune." He points at her attic dormer window. "I will prove that cash came from Daisy's safe. And when I do, you are going to jail."

Mary watches him disappear around the side of her house. Feeling dizzy, she stumbles over to the porch and sits down on the steps. Sensing her turmoil, Biscuit nudges up beside her, covering her face with licks.

Mary strokes his fur. "I don't understand it, buddy. I reckon I broke the spell by telling the chief about the tree. I didn't know I was meant to keep it a secret. Granted wishes should come with instructions. But I admit, I'm relieved. The adage is true. Money doesn't buy happiness. I'm grateful for the opportunity to fix up my house, but I'm no more or less happy than I was before the wish."

Mary's still sitting on the steps, talking out loud to the dog, when a stranger, an older woman with frizzy gray hair and hunched shoulders, sneaks around the side of the house.

Mary jumps to her feet, her hand pressed against her pounding heart. "Geez, you scared me. Can I help you with something?"

"I came to see the tree." The woman gestures at the maple. "Is that it?"

Mary tenses. "This is private property, ma'am. You need to leave." She takes the woman by the arm and walks her back to the gate.

Curiosity seekers arrive in droves. Some are bold enough to ring her doorbell, requesting a viewing of the tree. Others are sneaky. When she finds them hiding in her bushes and trying to straddle the fence in her backyard, Mary chases them away with her broom.

She locates two rusty padlocks in the garden shed and attaches them to the gates to keep the intruders out of the backyard. But there's little she can do to protect the front. They congregate on her lawn and the sidewalk, hoping for a glimpse of the tree. Positioning herself in a rocker on the front porch, through an old megaphone she finds in the attic, she repeats over and over, "There is nothing to see here. The spell is broken. The show is over. Please, go home."

Throughout the day, one group leaves and another arrives. Neighbors complain about the chaos, but the police do little to break up the crowd.

Mary wakes early the following morning to find money covering her backyard. She calls the police chief, insisting he come over immediately. But when he arrives, he stares blankly at the money. "What're you trying to pull, Ms. May?"

"What do you mean?" Mary sweeps an arm at the blanket of paper bills. "All this money fell from the tree last night."

He appears confused. "What money? I don't know what you're talking about?"

She bends over and scoops up an armful of bills, tossing them into the air. "Don't you see them?"

Norton's gaze shifts to her, his features softening as he studies her face. "The only thing I see is a lady in need of professional psychiatric help."

Mary's shoulders slump. "But I'm not crazy."

"This isn't over, Ms. May. I'll be in touch." He tips his hat to her and leaves through the side gate.

Mary retrieves her rake from the garden shed. While she works, she tries to wrap her mind around the situation. She's used Maple Money to buy clothes and a car and pay for services rendered on her house. The workmen and salespeople accepted the cash, no questions asked. The chief saw the money in the steamer trunk. Why can't he see it on the ground?

None of it makes any sense. Mary's head throbs from worrying about it. She's certain of only one thing: she hasn't heard the last from Chief Norton.

※

LATE ONE AFTERNOON at the end of the week, Mary is adding essential oils to dried flowers for potpourri when she receives a visit from Bess. "This is a surprise," she says.

"I came to apologize. I've been thinking a lot about what you said at the Fourth of July picnic." Bess gestures at the crowd gathered in the front yard. "Can we talk in private?"

"Sure." Mary opens the door wider. "Come on in. Would you like some lemonade?"

"That'd be great."

Bess follows Mary through the living room to the kitchen. "I've thought a lot about this kitchen over the years. All the meals we shared at this old farm table." She runs her hand over the worn pine wood. "Your mama was one hell of an excellent cook." She circles the room. "The natural sunlight spilling through all these windows really warms the space. Makes me feel all cozy inside."

"That's nice of you to say. Truth be told, the kitchen needs updating. But I can't bring myself to make the changes for fear of losing the ambiance."

Mary pours two glasses of lemonade, and they sit across from each other at the table, reminiscing about old times.

"I was hurt when you no longer wanted to be my friend," Bess says. "But I don't blame you. You were right. Evie and I weren't very nice to you back then. Instead of being sensitive about your infertility, we shoved our children in your face."

"That's all in the past now. Water under the bridge." Mary wants to believe Bess's apology is sincere, but she senses her old friend has an ulterior motive for being here.

Bess turns in her chair to look out at the backyard. "Is it true about the tree?"

Mary's blood runs cold. "Yes."

"My daughter needs braces. And we don't have the money to pay for them. Would you consider floating me a loan?"

Mary remembers the preteen girl from the Fourth of July picnic with crooked teeth. She sets down her lemonade and leaves the table. She races up to the attic, grabs several bundles of cash worth over five thousand dollars, and returns to the kitchen. She drops the bundles in a plastic grocery bag and hands it to Bess. "If your kid needs braces, she should have them." Mary gestures at the potpourri production on the counter. "I need to get back to work. I trust you can see yourself out."

"Thank you, Mary. This means so much." Bess drops the bag of money in her oversized purse and scurries out the front door.

Mary fights back tears. Bess didn't come for a visit or to apologize for the way she'd treated Mary all those years ago. She only wanted money. And Mary doesn't blame her. If she had a teenage daughter who needed braces, she'd do whatever was necessary to get them for her.

An hour later Evie rings her doorbell. Unlike Bess, Evie doesn't bother with pleasantries. She blurts, "My kid needs to have his tonsils out, and we can't afford the insurance deductible. Will you consider loaning us the money? Heck, why not give us the money since we're old friends and it's growing on a tree in your backyard?"

"Wait here. I'll be right back." Mary closes the front door and returns to the attic for more bundles of cash, giving Evie the same amount she gave Bess.

Mary doubts Evie's child needs his tonsils out. Her old friends are taking advantage of her windfall. But Mary has plenty to spare, and she doesn't mind giving away the money to those in need. She just hates being used. That familiar emptiness inside of her engulfs her.

CHAPTER 6

A photograph of Mary with her megaphone appears on the front page of the paper on Saturday morning. The headline reads, "Crazy Lady Lies about Money Tree." Mary doesn't bother reading the article. She stuffs the paper in the kitchen trash can and brews herself a cup of tea.

She takes her tea to the table on the back porch. Paper currency covers the yard, beckoning to her to get to work. But she's weary of the raking and the sorting and the counting.

Mary contemplates how her life has changed since the tree granted her wish. Aside from being able to make the house repairs, nothing good has come from the money. She was lonely before. She's still lonely. She has the same number of friends as before. Zero. She envied Daisy her beautiful wardrobe and fancy car. Now, Mary has a closet full of new clothes with nowhere to wear them. And her fancy car is too big, drinks too much gas, and is difficult to park.

There must be something more. What is she missing?

She drags herself out to the yard and retrieves her rake from the shed. She's only been working a few minutes when a voice calls out to her, "Hey, lady! Why are you raking the air?"

She looks around for the person belonging to the voice. She spots a man in the second-floor window at the house next door. He's wearing his bathrobe and waving a pair of binoculars at her. He's lived in the house for more than a year, and she hasn't yet met him, doesn't even know his name. Mary's a sorry excuse for a neighbor. Her mama would've marched over on his move-in day and presented him with a pineapple upside down cake to welcome him to the neighborhood.

She gestures at the piles of cash. "You can't see all this?"

"Nah. And neither can you. See a shrink, lady," he says, and slams the window shut.

Mary looks up at the maple. *Am I losing my mind? Or are you playing a trick on me?* The wind rustles the tree's branches, and more paper bills float down.

Mary reluctantly returns to her work. She has more money than she can ever spend. How can she make the tree stop producing?

After completing her chores, she spends the rest of the morning running errands. People point at her and laugh everywhere she goes—the market, the pet store, the dry cleaners. She's the town pariah, the crazy lady with the money tree. She's unloading the groceries from the Range Rover when an idea pops into her head. Why not simply reverse the wish?

Once she puts the groceries away, she sits down at the kitchen table and jots a note on her stationery. *I wish my maple tree would stop producing money.* She fastens a leash to Biscuit's collar, and they stroll over to the town square, where Mary attaches her note to the Wishing Tree with a satin ribbon.

She walks with a lighter step on the way home. The tree

will grant her wish, and her life will go back to normal. She'll no longer have to wake at the crack of dawn and spend hours collecting, counting, and stashing the cash. But what will she do with her free time? Perhaps she'll get a job at one of the trendy boutiques on Main Street. On second thought, no one will hire the crazy lady with the money tree. Now may be the right time to start her potpourri and tea business.

Back at home, she retreats to her basement, where large plastic containers of lavender and rose potpourri line the storage shelves. She began this new hobby at the end of last summer. She perfected the process over the winter, and she now has more potpourri than she knows what to do with. The farmers' market seems the most logical place to sell it. But what if no one will buy it? Since she's no longer strapped for cash, why not give it away?

She scoops potpourri into clear cellophane bags and ties them with colorful ribbon. She spends hours creating a logo on her computer—clusters of lavender and roses with the name of her new company, Invisible Garden, in gold cursive. She prints out sheets of labels, attaching one to each bag, and places the bags in a cardboard box for easy transport.

It's nearing dinnertime when she emerges from the basement with her box. Pouring gazpacho into a bowl and peach iced tea into a glass, she takes her dinner out to the porch to watch the sunset. She waits until after dark before sneaking around to the neighboring homes and leaving a bag at each front door.

Contentment overcomes Mary as she walks home with her empty box. She worked hard creating the potpourri. So what if her efforts didn't earn her any money? Giving the lovely scented flower petals away as secret gifts is way more meaningful.

A VIOLENT STORM blows through Linden Falls during the night. Lightning streaks across the dark sky and loud claps of thunder bring a terrified Biscuit scampering to Mary's room. She rubs the whimpering dog's back. "There, now. The storm will pass in a minute."

But the storm rages for hours. Mary and Biscuit cuddle together under the covers. She flinches, and he whines every time lightning cracks. The wind rattles and sways the old maple. The tree creaks and groans, and more than once during the long night, she considers moving to the basement in case it crashes down on the house.

When the worst of the storm moves out, Mary and Biscuit manage a few hours of restless sleep. When they wake at dawn, Mary throws back the covers and changes into work clothes. Her yard will be wrecked from the storm, but if luck is on her side, her wish was granted and there will be no money to collect.

With Biscuit on her heels, she goes downstairs and out the kitchen door to the screen porch. She takes in the sight before her. Paper money covers every square inch of her yard. Grass. Mulch. Gravel paths. She walks down the porch stairs and steps ankle deep into wet cash.

Is Mary responsible for this surplus? Did her wish anger the tree gods? She looks heavenward. Someone up there is trying to tell her something. Tears of frustration leak from her eyes. Her wish was denied. She'll have to sell the house to get rid of the tree. She thinks about the money she gave Bess and Evie for their children's braces and tonsillectomy. And the satisfaction of secretly delivering the potpourri to her neighbors. An idea comes to mind, and a glimmer of hope takes ahold of her heart.

"That's it!" Mary's feet leave the ground as she punches the air. "That's what the tree is trying to tell me!"

She goes to the shed for the rake and wheelbarrow. The

process is tedious. After wheeling loads of wet cash to the porch, she transfers it to laundry baskets and carries the baskets inside to the laundry room. She remains in the laundry room while the dryer is running for fear it might catch on fire. After the drying cycle ends, she stuffs the crisp bills into black trash bags and starts the process all over again.

Lunchtime has come and gone by the time the lawn is cleared and the money dried and stored in old suitcases in the attic. Mary is starving, but she doesn't take time to eat. She drives over to the florist on the square. The shelves are empty aside from a lone teddy bear announcing the arrival of a baby boy. There are no potted plants—not even a Spathiphyllum. One pitiful-looking bouquet of wildflowers remains in a bucket of water in the self-serve refrigerator.

"Do you have any more flowers in the back?" Mary asks the gentleman behind the counter.

"Not yet. Hopefully, by later this afternoon. The storm delayed my shipment."

"That storm was a doozy," Mary says, remembering the harrowing night she spent with Biscuit. She removes the bouquet from the bucket and approaches the counter. The man is about her age with a full head of sandy hair and a smile that reaches his deep blue eyes. "Do you have any containers for sale?"

"I do, but I would have to charge you double the price I pay the wholesaler. You're better off getting them from the craft store."

Mary narrows her eyes at him. "Better not let your boss hear you telling a customer to shop somewhere else."

He thumbs his chest. "I *am* the boss."

"Oh." Mary's gaze shifts to the name Bertie's Petals scrawled in yellow-green paint on the window. "Is Bertie your wife?"

"My wife's grandmother. The shop's been in the family for generations. My wife, Alice, passed away from cancer two years ago. This shop meant everything to her. After her diagnosis, I took an early retirement from my law firm, and we hired a floral designer. The floral designer quit on me last week. She just up and moved to New York with no notice. I enjoy running the business and interacting with the customers, but I'm not the creative type. You wouldn't by any chance be looking for a job?"

"Sorry. I have all the work I can handle at the moment. About those containers... I'm in a bit of a rush. I'll take three."

He disappears into the back and returns with three nice-size cylinder vases. He adds up the items and tells her the amount. She removes three twenties from her wallet, and he gives her the change. "You look familiar. Have you shopped in here before?"

"Not that I remember. I grow my own flowers. But the storm ruined them."

He looks more closely at her. "I swear I've seen you somewhere before. Wait, a minute." He wags his finger at her. "You're that money tree lady."

She grunts in response.

"I'm curious. Does the tree shed money like it does leaves in the fall?"

She narrows her eyes. Is that a smirk on his lips? "Are you making fun of me?"

"Not at all. I'm fascinated."

"Why? No one else believes me."

"I'm an attorney. I believe in someone's innocence until they're proven guilty. Besides, even a pathological liar couldn't make up a story that crazy."

Mary bursts out laughing. "Tell that to Chief Norton."

"Right. I read about Daisy Crawford's accusations. I don't know why anyone would believe her."

"Her husband is an important man in this town."

The man leans across the counter. "So, let me get this straight. You tied a wish to the Wishing Tree, and voilà, money starts dropping like leaves from your maple."

Mary hesitates, deciding how much to tell him. His warm smile makes her trust him. "There's more to it than that. I made the wish on a whim. I wasn't really asking for money. I was mocking the tree for wishes I'd made in the past that didn't come true."

Sadness falls over his face. "I know how that goes."

Mary's heart goes out to him. He probably asked the tree to cure his wife. "It's the darnedest thing. People can see the money when I pay cash for something. Like just now. The tree shed those three twenties I gave you for the flowers and containers. But it appears only I can see the money when it falls from the tree."

"Hmm." He drums his fingers on the counter as he considers this. "That is strange. And you don't know why?"

"Nope. This is all very confusing." Mary leaves the counter and goes to the window, staring out across the square at the tree. "My wish has become something of a nuisance. I paid a visit to the Wishing Tree yesterday, asking it to stop the maple from making money. I can't say for sure whether the tree caused the storm, but there was more cash in my yard this morning than ever before."

"So instead of stopping production, it put out a surplus," he says. "Like it was admonishing you for wishing the tree would stop."

"Something like that. Although I don't think the Wishing Tree was punishing me for being ungrateful. I think the tree" —she glances upward—"or somebody up there is sending me a message." Mary turns her back to the window and faces him again. "I'm meant to be doing something meaningful with the money. Like giving it away to people in need." She returns to the counter. "Would you like some to tide you over until you hire a floral designer?"

He chuckles. "I'm fine. But thank you. How're you planning to go about giving the money away? If you announce it in the paper, you're liable to have a stampede on your hands."

Mary creases her brow. "I'm still figuring out the details."

"I have faith that you will." He comes from behind the counter. "If the rumors are true, Chief Norton is working with the county's district attorney to build a case against you. While I'm no longer practicing law, I would be happy to offer advice." He holds out his hand. "By the way, I'm Phillip Steele. My friends call me Phil."

She takes his hand in hers. His skin is soft against her calloused palm. "And I'm Mary May. First and last, not double."

He tilts his head to the side. "Really? I think Mary May suits you as a double name."

Mary smiles shyly. "You can call me whatever you like." She gathers her purchases into her arms. "I hope I don't need legal advice, but I appreciate your offer. Unless you want the entire town thinking you're as crazy as me, I suggest you keep this conversation to yourself."

He walks with her to the front of the shop and opens the door for her. "Let them think what they want. I believe you, Mary May. One day, I'd like to come see your tree."

CHAPTER 7

Mary chooses the freshest blooms from the bouquet of wildflowers and discards the rest. She adds sprigs of herbs and greenery from her yard to make three small arrangements. She folds wads of hundred-dollar bills into small envelopes, adheres her Invisible Garden logo, and attaches the envelope to a plastic card pick. She delivers her arrangements to the lady in the wheelchair around the corner, the homeless woman camped out on the park bench in the square, and the neighbor who wears a kerchief over her bald head whom Mary suspects is battling cancer. Only the homeless woman sees Mary, and she flashes Mary a toothless grin when presented with the flowers.

Mary returns home in high spirits. Not only has she determined what the tree gods intended for the money, at long last, she has finally discovered her purpose in life.

She reads a chapter in her current romance novel while eating a chicken Caesar salad on the porch. When she's finished reading, she moves to a rocker and rests her head against the back, closing her eyes as exhaustion sets in. She overhears two women, out for an evening stroll, when they pass by on the sidewalk.

"Someone left a bag of potpourri at my door last night," one woman says. "The mixture smells heavenly."

"I got one too," the other woman says. "My house smells like a summer rose garden."

Mary smiles to herself. She's glad the women received their gifts. She felt certain the potpourri bags had blown away in the storm.

Her thoughts drift to Phil. He must have loved Alice very much to give up his law career to take care of her business when she fell ill. Mary wonders how many times he asked the Wishing Tree to save his wife. Certainly no more than Mary asked the tree to give her a baby.

After completing her chores the following morning, Mary heads over to the used car dealership and trades in the Range Rover for the slate-blue pickup truck. She feels more like herself behind the wheel as she drives off the lot. On the way home, she stops in at the garden shop at Duncan's Hardware for a bag of wildflower seed mix. She spends the afternoon digging up the remaining grass in her backyard, preparing the soil, and sprinkling a mixture of wildflower seeds and sand on top. Because it's late in the season to be planting seeds, magic is needed to make them grow. She walks over to the town square and pins a wish to the tree, asking the tree to please make her garden bountiful. She wakes the next day to find rows of gorgeous blooms—zinnias, daisies, and brown-eyed Susans among the many varieties.

Mary searches local gift shops and novelty stores for small bowls, large coffee mugs, and vases in all shapes and sizes. She loads up on floral supplies from the craft store and organizes them in the kitchen. She moves her mahogany pedestal table out of the way and has a commercial refrigerator installed in the dining room. And by the end of the third week in July, she's ready to get down to business.

Mary scours the *Linden Falls Gazette* and tunes into the local news stations on her archaic television in the kitchen for tidbits about the citizens of Linden Falls who are down on their luck. Those who have lost their jobs and those filing for bankruptcy. The ones who are sick or hospitalized or have been injured in an automobile accident. She eats lunch at the Crooked Porch Café every day, listening to the gossip floating from nearby tables. There is no shortage of people needing a bouquet to cheer them up and a wad of cash to make their circumstances less stressful.

Mary has little time for herself between maintaining her yard, creating arrangements, and making deliveries. But she's never been happier. She remains incognito by wearing oversized sunglasses and a large floppy straw hat when delivering the arrangements. But Linden Falls is a small town, and it's only a matter of time before someone identifies her.

For the first time since making the wish, Mary doesn't have to worry about hiding the money. Whatever she collects, she gives away.

On Friday of the last week in July, Mary returns from making deliveries to find Jodi waiting on her front porch.

"I'm here to warn you about Daisy," Jodi says.

Mary drops to the chair next to her. "What about Daisy?"

"She's out to get you, Mary. She's determined to send you to jail."

"But I didn't take anything from her safe. The tree . . . Never mind. It's hard to explain. You wouldn't understand."

Jodi angles her body toward Mary. "I might if you tried me. Money growing on trees is farfetched, but I had a similar experience with the Wishing Tree years ago. Sometimes granted wishes end up being curses."

Mary throws her hands up. "As the saying goes, *Careful what you wish for.*"

"Exactly." Jodi stands up and walks to the edge of the porch, looking out across the front yard. "I told Daisy I believed you about the tree."

Mary's mouth drops open. "Why would you do that when you hardly know me?"

"Because I know Daisy. And I know what she's capable of. She went ballistic on me when I took your side. Now she's trying to destroy me as well. She got my husband fired from his job." Jodi turns to face Mary. "My husband has been a project manager for Daisy's husband for nearly twenty years. Frank never missed a single day. Even when he had the flu, he showed up for work. Now, because of my fight with Daisy, Bob Crawford fired Frank."

Anger flashes through Mary. "Of all the rotten things to do."

Jodi's chin quivers. "When Frank pressed him about it, Bob said he was making some changes. But we all know it's because of his wife. What Daisy wants, Daisy gets."

"Don't I know it." Mary goes to stand beside Jodi at the railing. "I'm so sorry, Jodi. I feel terrible about this."

"It's not your fault," Jodi sobs. "It's mine. Frank was a carpenter when we were first married. I dreamed of belonging to the country club and being friends with society women, so I asked the tree to find my husband a higher-paying job. Daisy's husband hired him the next day. His job has been a blessing. But also a—"

"Curse," Mary says, finishing her sentence.

Jodi nods. "Same goes for Daisy. She has made my life easier in some ways, and in others, she's made it a living hell," she says, crying so hard her shoulders heave.

"You poor thing. Come inside." Taking her by the arm, Mary walks Jodi inside to the living room.

Other than Bess, Mary hasn't had a guest in her home in years. She spends most of her time in the kitchen. She can't remember the last time she sat in the living room. She doesn't even know if the television still works. But instead of feeling awkward sitting next to this stranger on the sofa, she feels oddly comfortable. Even though the woman is bawling her eyes out.

She offers Jodi a box of tissues. Jodi takes one, blows her nose, and cries harder. When Jodi's breathing begins to spasm, Mary goes to the kitchen for some iced tea. "Here, drink this. It'll make you feel better."

Jodi takes a sip between hiccups. "This is superb. What kind of tea is it?"

"My special blend of peach tea."

Jodi draws in big gulps of air until the tears stop flowing and her breathing steadies. She guzzles down the tea. Tapping her fingernail to the empty glass, she says, "You should market this. It's delicious."

If she can figure out how to package it, maybe she'll give away her tea with the flowers and potpourri.

Jodi sets the glass on the coffee table and settles back on the sofa. "I'm sorry I fell apart on you like that. I don't know what got into me. I can't remember when I've cried so hard."

Mary squeezes Jodi's shoulder. "You've been keeping your emotions locked away. You needed to let them out. Talking about it might help. Is your husband terribly upset about his job?"

Pressing the tissue to her nose, Jodi shakes her head. "Frank confessed that he's stayed at Crawford Custom Homes all these years because of me. He didn't want me to lose the lifestyle I'd grown accustomed to. And I stayed in the friendship with Daisy because I didn't want him to lose the job he loved so much. But he never loved that job. Apparently, Bob is as difficult to work for as Daisy is to be friends with."

Mary's heart goes out to this woman. "Do you need any money to tide you over until he finds another job?"

"No. But thanks. I couldn't take a handout. We'll be fine. We have savings. Frank already has a lead on another job."

"How about a part-time job for *you* in the meantime?" The words slip from Mary's tongue before she thinks about them. But the arrangement makes sense. And it would solve both their problems.

The lines in Jodi's forehead deepen. "What kind of job?"

"Delivering flower arrangements. I've been giving flowers and money to sick people and folks down on their luck. But shh!" Mary holds a finger to her lips. "Don't tell anyone. I'm trying to keep it a secret."

Jodi's brown eyes widen. "That's you? You're the Flower Angel? I volunteer in the gift shop at the hospital twice a week. I heard some nurses talking about how much your generous gifts mean to the patients." She gives Mary's arm a playful slap. "That's one way to solve your money problem."

Mary beams. "The money I collect in the backyard in the morning goes out the front door in the afternoon."

"You have a big heart, Mary May. I totally want in. You don't even have to pay me."

"I insist on paying you. Believe me, you'll be earning it. Delivering flowers in the heat of the summer is hard work. Besides, you'll be doing me a favor. So far, I've hidden my identity by wearing hats and sunglasses. But people are getting curious. You can simply say the donor wishes to remain anonymous.

"That makes sense." Jodi jumps to her feet. "I'm so excited. I can't wait to tell Frank. When can I start?"

Mary stands to face her. "Tomorrow afternoon. Can you be here around one o'clock?"

Jodi bobs her head. "With bells on."

Mary walks Jodi to the door and watches her walk down the sidewalk to her car. Mary has a tingling feeling all over. Is it possible she just made a new friend? Something tells her her life just changed for the better.

CHAPTER 8

*J*odi arrives for work before noon the following day. "I hope you don't mind me coming early. I have too much time on my hands these days. And I'm eager to get started."

"I admire your enthusiasm. Come on in. I was just getting ready to make some tea," Mary says, motioning for Jodi to follow her to the kitchen.

Jodi pauses in the doorway, gaping at the buckets of flowers scattered about the kitchen. "Where on earth did you get all these gorgeous blooms?"

"Believe it or not, they came out of my yard." Mary pours water into the kettle and sets it on the stove.

Jodi fingers the petal of a pink peony. "What about these? Peonies don't bloom this time of year."

Mary flashes a mischievous grin. "They do in my yard. I forgot to tell you about my second Wishing Tree wish."

"Are you joking? You are a glutton for punishment."

Mary snorts out a laugh. "You'd think I'd learn my lesson. My second wish could very well turn out to be a curse as well." When the tea finishes steeping, Mary brings the mugs and a plate of shortbread cookies over to the table.

Jodi joins her at the table. "Tell me about the wish. I'm dying to hear."

"I needed more flowers for my arrangements, so I bought a bag of wildflower seeds at the hardware store. Since it's so late in the season, I needed a little help to make them grow. I wished for a bountiful garden. Now everything in my yard is on steroids."

Jodi turns around in her chair and looks out across the porch at the yard. "Whoa. It's *Alice in Wonderland.*"

"It's like magic. I cut them, and they grow back almost immediately."

Jodi bites into a shortbread cookie. "How do you identify the recipients of your arrangements? Your donees, if that's even a word."

Mary smiles. "It is. I looked it up in the dictionary." Grabbing a handful of flowers, she cuts off the tips of their stems and arranges them in a vase. "I find most of them in the *Gazette* and on the local evening news. I welcome suggestions if you have any."

"I know the secretary at my church. I could ask her for the parishioner sick list."

Mary looks up from her flowers. "That's a great idea. We can ask other churches as well."

"What about social media?" Jodi flashes a wicked grin. "We can stalk people we know, to find out if they're having problems."

"I'll leave the stalking to you. I stay away from social media at all costs."

"I'm on it," Jodi says and goes on about the various social media sites she frequents. While she talks, she picks a few choice blooms out of a bucket and arranges them with some greenery and herbs in a vase, tying a cheerful bow around the neck. "There." She pushes the vase toward Mary. "One down. How many more to go?"

"Twenty." Mary examines Jodi's creation. "You're really good at this. Your job description just got bigger."

"Arranging flowers is one of my favorite things." Jodi lets out a sigh. "I trip over my own feet on the tennis court. I get bored easily when shopping. Going out to lunch every day is bad for my waistline. But garden club is the one thing I truly enjoyed in my former life."

"Who says you have to give up garden club?"

"Daisy." Jodi reaches for another vase. "Our president notified me last night. They're kicking me out."

Mary presses her lips thin. "You can't let them treat you this way, Jodi. You need to stand up for yourself. Fight for your rights."

"I would if it was worth fighting for. But I no longer wish to associate with those women. Maybe I'll start my own garden club. I'll start small with just the two of us."

Mary's heart warms at the idea of being in any kind of club with Jodi. Even if it is just the two of them.

Mary and Jodi chatter on as they work, discussing gardening and home improvement projects and the other hobbies they have in common, like reading and knitting. It's past twelve o'clock by the time the arrangements are ready for delivery.

Jodi stands and stretches. "I guess I'd better get going if I'm going to deliver all these today."

"Not until you've eaten lunch. How does chicken salad sound?"

"Perfect. Can I help?"

"You can pour the tea. The pitcher's in the refrigerator." Mary places a healthy scoop of homemade chicken salad on two plates, adding thick slices of red juicy tomatoes and some bread and butter pickle chips.

Jodi takes a bite of chicken salad and lets out a groan. "This is delicious. The tarragon and grapes are a nice addition. Did you make it?"

"I did," Mary says, forking off a bite of tomato.

"You're a marvel, Mary May. You grow beautiful flowers. You're an amazing cook. Is there anything you can't do?"

Mary stares down at her plate. "I'm not very good at friendships."

"I don't believe that. Maybe you haven't found the right women to be friends with yet."

Tears blur Mary's vision. She wants so much to be friends with Jodi. But Jodi is worldly, and Mary is plain Jane. Jodi is used to having lots of friends and an active social life. Mary is more accustomed to staying at home, alone.

Despite Mary's misgivings, a comfortable companionship quickly develops between the two women. Two days later, on the first Monday in August, Jodi arrives early, while Mary is still raking up money.

"My word! Would you look at all that cash?"

Mary stops raking and looks up. "You mean, you can see it? Most people can't."

Jodi frowns. "That's strange. I wonder why?"

Mary tosses up her hands. "It's a mystery. I can't figure it out."

Jodi comes down off the porch and traipses through the piles of cash. "This is a lot of work for one person. Do you have another rake?"

"Should be one in there," Mary says, gesturing at the garden shed.

For the rest of the week, Jodi arrives before dawn to help with the outside work. They eat lunch together before Jodi heads out with the deliveries and Mary spends the afternoon taking care of administrative work. At the end of every day, when Jodi returns from making deliveries, they spend a few minutes together on the porch drinking tea or lemonade.

On Friday, Jodi brings a bottle of prosecco with her to work and places it in Mary's refrigerator to chill. When Mary questions her about it, Jodi says, "It's a surprise for later."

That afternoon, when Jodi finishes with her delivery rounds, she pops the cork and pours two glasses. "Let's have our celebration on the porch."

Mary follows Jodi out to the front porch. "What're we celebrating?"

"Life." Jodi clinks Mary's glass. "This job has given my life new purpose. And I am eternally grateful to you. After Daisy dumped me, I wasn't sure how I would occupy my time. But I'm having the most fun ever. For the first time in years, I'm doing something meaningful."

Mary takes a sip and raises her glass to Jodi. "We're doing good work. Here's to our partnership."

"To our partnership," Jodi repeats and adds, "And to our friendship. You're different from my other friends."

Mary's smile fades. *Different. Just as she suspected.*

"What's wrong, Mary? We are friends, aren't we?"

Mary doesn't respond.

"I enjoy spending time with you," Jodi says in a wounded tone. "I assumed you felt the same."

"I told you I'm not good at friendships." Mary stares down at her champagne. "But the truth is, I've been burned in the past by women I thought were my friends."

"Me too! In the worst way. In my previous life, what I now refer to as my fake life, I was surrounded by women who claimed to be my friends. On the tennis courts. At garden club meetings and lunches. But I always felt out of place when I was with them. Those women are not nice people. Some are downright vicious. Believe it or not, they gossip about their own children."

Mary's jaw goes slack. "That's awful."

"It is awful. But you saved me from all that fakeness. Daisy was right about you. You're the real deal, Mary May."

Little hairs stand to attention at the back of Mary's neck. "What exactly did Daisy say about me?"

"She once told me you were a good listener. That you were a genuine person with a big heart. And she was right."

"I'm shocked. I never heard Daisy compliment anyone."

"I consider you my friend, Mary. I hope one day you'll feel the same way about me." Jodi pours more bubbling liquid into their glasses. "Can I ask you a personal question?"

"Of course," Mary says, relieved to be off the subject of friendship.

"Why did you divorce your husband?"

"I couldn't have children, so Orville found someone who could."

Jodi presses her lips thin. "I figured it was something like that. You're beautiful and talented, a wonderful woman with much to offer. Why haven't you gotten remarried?"

Mary shrugs. "I haven't met the right man yet, I guess. Although, truth be told, I haven't been looking. I'm happy on my own."

"Sounds lonely to me. No friends. No man. No . . ." Jodi stops herself.

Was she going to say *children*?

"I don't mind being alone. I actually prefer flying solo," Mary says in a half-hearted tone.

"Frank's brother divorced last year. He's a wonderful guy. His wife was not a wonderful woman. He's struggling, and I think you would be a breath of fresh air for him. Would you consider going on a blind date with him?"

Mary hesitates before answering. "Maybe. I'd have to think about it."

"The two of you would make a cute—" Jodi stops in mid-sentence at the sight of a police car parking on the curb in front of Mary's house.

"Uh-oh. I have a bad feeling about this," Mary says under her breath.

"What's going on?" Jodi asks.

"I don't know. But we're about to find out."

Two officers get out of the patrol car, and as they walk toward her, Mary stands to greet them. Out of the corner of her eye, she notices her neighbors congregating on the sidewalk across the street.

The taller of the officers looks back and forth between the two women. "Is one of you Mary Ellis May?"

Mary places her hand on her chest. "I'm Mary. What can I do for you?"

"You're under arrest for grand larceny." He removes a set of handcuffs from his belt and grabs her by the arm.

Mary jerks her arm away. "You don't need to manhandle me. I'll come willingly with you. Please, don't cause a scene in front of my neighbors."

The officer says, "Fine. But don't try anything funny."

Jodi walks alongside them out to the patrol car. "How can I help, Mary? What do you want me to do?"

"Get in touch with Phil Steele at Bertie's Petals," Mary says. "He's an attorney. He'll know how to handle it."

CHAPTER 9

Mary spends a lonely night in a holding cell. The police won't tell her anything more about the charges or allow her the one allotted phone call. The orange jumpsuit they make her wear irritates her skin, and she's terrified to touch anything in the cell. The pillow is flat as a pancake and stains from bodily fluids of previous occupants cover the mattress. Mary sits on the cold concrete floor with her knees tucked under her chin. She refuses to cry. She didn't steal anything from anyone, and innocent people don't go to prison.

To avoid thinking about her predicament, she ponders her discussion with Jodi about friendship. More than anything, she wants to be Jodi's friend. What must Jodi think of Mary now, being hauled off by the police like a common criminal? What happens if Daisy apologizes to Jodi, and Jodi returns to her old life? Mary will be all alone again. And the emptiness will gnaw away at her insides, creating a deeper and darker void.

Should she go on a blind date with Jodi's brother-in-law? It's been so long, she wouldn't know how to act. Mary has thought little about falling in love again. She's happy on her own. Or is she? Is there a special someone out there somewhere searching for her? Mary thinks about Daisy's active social life. The world is passing Mary by. And it's her own fault. She's been hiding out in her house, moving through the motions of life without really living.

Curled in a ball on the hard floor, Mary dozes off and on throughout the endless night. A female guard wakes her with a bowl of watery oatmeal around seven. "May I make my phone call now?" Mary asks in a meek voice.

"Sorry. Chief says you have to wait."

"Wait for what?"

The guard hunches a beefy shoulder. "No clue. You'll have to ask him."

At nine o'clock, a different female guard comes for her. "Your attorney is here for you. He'll be taking you to your meeting with the magistrate."

The guard handcuffs Mary and walks her through a series of hallways to the reception area where Phil Steele is waiting, looking sharp in a slim-fitting navy suit, crisp white shirt, and a blue-and-red-striped tie. While Mary hardly knows him, she's enormously relieved to see him.

"Thank you so much for coming," she says.

"I wish I could've gotten here sooner." Phil looks over at the guard. "Are the cuffs really necessary?"

"Yes, sir. I'm just following protocol. I'll be escorting you to the courthouse."

On the way across the street, Phil explains, "Judge Chambers is a friend of mine. He's hopping mad about being dragged down to the courthouse on a Saturday morning. But he's in no position to argue. The police had no business arresting you on a Friday afternoon."

"Then why did they?" Mary asks.

"I have a hunch. But we'll talk more about that after the

arraignment. This shouldn't take long. The judge has a tee time at ten." They reach the courthouse, and Phil holds the door open for her. "Let me do the talking. When the judge asks, you plead not guilty."

"Got it," Mary says with a curt nod.

The arraignment takes less than five minutes. After Mary pleads not guilty, the judge sets bail and a date at the end of the month to hear her case in court. Phil arranges for bail, and they return to the police station, where she goes through the process of being released.

"I'll give you a ride home," Phil says, and leads Mary to his Tahoe in the parking lot.

The interior smells woodsy, like a walk in the forest on a fall day. She's disappointed to see a pink hair scrunchy in the cupholder. Phil must have a girlfriend. Not that a handsome and successful man like Phil would have anything to do with a jailbird.

"I'm so worried about Biscuit. He must be beside himself," Mary says, more to herself than Phil as they leave the parking lot.

"Don't worry about Biscuit. Jodi wanted me to be sure to tell you she took him home with her last night."

"The police wouldn't tell me anything about the charges. They wouldn't even allow me a phone call."

Phil tightens his grip on the steering wheel. "Something smells very fishy about this case. I was up half the night making phone calls. I spoke with the district attorney. They are charging you with grand larceny. Daisy Crawford claims you stole over twenty thousand dollars and a diamond tennis bracelet from her."

"Her diamond tennis bracelet? That's a boldface lie. I'm not a thief. I never took anything from their house. Not even one of her expensive bottled waters."

"They have a list of salespeople and contractors who will

testify that you paid cash for high-dollar items like sports cars and home improvement."

Mary gulps back a wave of fear. "That's all true. I got the money from the tree. What's your hunch about the Friday afternoon arrest?"

"My gut tells me Bob Crawford had something to do with it. He and Chief Norton are buddies. The idea was for you to spend the weekend in jail. Which is what would've happened if I hadn't gotten Judge Chambers involved. I consider this obstruction of justice, and I aim to get to the bottom of it. Unless you know someone, I'm happy to recommend a good criminal attorney. There are a couple in my old firm."

Her neck snaps as she looks over at him. "But I thought *you* were representing me."

Phil smiles at her. "I'm flattered. But I'm rusty. It's been years since I practiced law."

Mischief tugs at her lips. "I'll pay you in cash."

He laughs out loud. "I'm tempted. I relish the opportunity to stick it to Chief Norton and Bob Crawford. I don't like underhanded dealings. Especially when it involves our law enforcement agencies. Problem is, I don't have the time."

"Could you make the time? I'll do whatever it takes. I'll even manage Bertie's Petals for you."

Phil chews on this for a minute. "I guess I could spare a few hours of my day now that Lily's working part-time at the shop."

Lily? Mary's gaze shifts to the hair scrunchy. She imagines a petite woman with long blonde hair working behind the counter at Bertie's. Does Lily arrange flowers? Or is her job to take orders and process charges?

"Is that a yes?" Mary asks.

"On one condition."

Mary furrows her brow. "What's that?"

Phil turns onto her street and parks behind her truck in the driveway. "You let me see the maple tree."

"Deal." Mary suspects he's testing her. Because she's desperate for his help, she goes along with him.

They get out of the car, and she shows him inside to the kitchen. "Would you like some hot tea?"

"No, thanks. I had coffee earlier." Phil goes to the back door and peers out the window.

Mary crosses her fingers and holds her breath, waiting for his reaction.

"Whoa! I don't believe it."

The air gushes out of her lungs. *He can see it!*

Phil prattles on. "Not that I didn't believe you. I'm an excellent judge of character. And you strike me as an honest woman. It's just . . ." His voice trails off.

"I understand. It's a lot to grasp."

"Does the tree drop this much every morning?"

"At least this much," Mary says. "Sometimes it's more."

He unlocks the door and steps out onto the porch. Mary goes to stand beside him.

Phil appears amazed. "When you mentioned growing your own flowers, I imagined a small bed with a few rose bushes. Not a flower farm."

Mary laughs. "My hobby got a little out of hand."

They walk out into the yard and wade through the flowers to the tree.

Phil kicks at the paper money and bills fly in the air. "How much do you think is here?"

"Ten thousand is the usual haul. I've gotten as much as thirty in one day. But that was before I planted all these flowers. Now money only drops at the base of the tree."

He turns in a circle as he takes it all in. "What do you do with the flowers?"

"It's a secret." Mary picks up a hundred-dollar bill and hands it to him. "Here."

He eyes the money, but he doesn't take it. "What's that for?"

"It's your retainer. I need official attorney-client privilege for what I'm about to tell you."

He snickers and takes the money. "I'm almost afraid to hear it."

"It's not a big deal, really. I just prefer to remain anonymous. I create arrangements and give the flowers and some cash to the sick and downtrodden."

"Ah-ha. When I heard about the Flower Angel, I thought it might be you. That day in my shop, you were searching for a way to use the money to help others. Your plan is brilliant."

The screen door bangs open, and Biscuit races toward her, trampling the flowers in his path.

Mary leans down to pet him, and he covers her face in licks. "Hey, buddy. I missed you too."

Jodi emerges from the porch with the morning paper tucked under her arm. Mary smiles at her. "Hey, Jodi. Thanks for taking care of Biscuit last night."

"My pleasure," Jodi says, massaging Biscuit's ears. "He was a gracious houseguest. He has excellent manners."

Mary gestures at her attorney. "You've met Phil."

Jodi smiles at him. "I got to Bertie's Petals in the nick of time yesterday, just as he was closing up shop for the day." She turns to Mary. "I'm so sorry this happened to you. Did you have to spend the night in jail?"

"Unfortunately. Daisy claims I stole twenty thousand dollars and a tennis bracelet from her."

Jodi's brown eyes pop out of her head. "That's a lie. I was with Daisy when she lost that bracelet at the Fourth of July picnic. Remember, she ran into you and spilled punch down the front of her white dress. I got her some fresh clothes from her house, and she changed in the restroom at the Crooked Porch. The next morning, she discovered the bracelet was missing. We spent the entire day looking for it. Daisy was frantic. She was worried about telling Bob. And now she doesn't have to, because you provided her with the perfect excuse. The conniving little bitch."

"Would you be willing to testify to that?" Phil asks.

"Damn straight. Unfortunately, there's more bad news." Jodi hands Mary the newspaper. "I have a feeling Daisy is responsible for this."

Mary opens the paper to find a photograph of herself being driven away in the patrol car. The headline reads: "Money Tree Lady Charged with Grand Larceny."

When she shows Phil the paper, he takes it from her and walks it over to the outdoor trash can. "Don't worry, Mary. We'll sort this out. Daisy and Bob Crawford will get what's coming to them. For the time being, keep your chin up and continue bringing joy to people's lives with your Angel Flowers."

A wave of determination overcomes her. "You're right. No good will come from fretting about this." She looks over at Jodi. "We need to get to work. We've already lost the better part of the morning."

When Mary and Jodi head to the garden shed, Phil follows on their heels. "It'll go quicker if I help."

"I can't ask you to do that," Mary says. "You've already done so much. Besides, you're wearing a suit."

"I insist." Phil takes off his suit coat and hangs it on the shed's doorknob. "I can't possibly turn down an opportunity to rake up cash." He grabs a rake from inside the shed, and the threesome gets to work.

The job goes much faster with Phil pitching in. Within an hour, the money is collected and the flowers cut.

Phil places a hand on his lower back, revealing damp armpits. "About that offer of tea. Can we put some ice in it?"

Mary laughs. "You've got it."

They transfer the cash to the laundry baskets, hauling them and the buckets of flowers into the kitchen. Mary pours three glasses of tea, and they stand in a circle gulping it down.

Jodi drops to a chair at the table. "I'm still stewing over what Daisy is doing to you. We need to figure out a way to catch her in her lie."

Phil drains the last of his tea and sets his glass on the counter. "That's my cue to leave. As Mary's attorney, I can't be privy to anything unethical or illegal."

Mary cuts her eyes at Jodi. "We're not doing anything unethical or illegal."

"I'm just trying to keep you out of jail," Jodi says.

Mary stomach hardens as the reality of a potential prison sentence sinks in. When she walks Phil to the door, she asks, "Do you really think there's a chance I'll have to serve time?"

"Not if I have anything to do with it." Phil gives her arm a squeeze. "Try not to worry. I'll get in touch with the district attorney first thing on Monday, and we'll go from there."

When she returns to the kitchen, Jodi is chewing on her lower lip while stuffing flowers into a vase.

Mary sits down opposite her. "Easy on the flowers, Jodi. You'll break the stems. What's on your mind?"

"I'm thinking I should make up with Daisy," Jodi says, her eyes on her work. "She'll forgive me if I beg her. She needs me. The rest of her friends don't kowtow to her like I did. You know how Daisy loves to brag. In a couple of days, Daisy will start running her mouth about framing you for theft. If I get her on tape, you're off the hook."

Cold dread settles over Mary. "Is that what you want? To be friends with Daisy again?"

Jodi looks up from the flowers. "Of course not. But it's the only thing I can think of to get the charges dropped."

"I'm sorry, Jodi, but I can't let you put yourself through the humiliation of begging for Daisy's forgiveness. We have to trust the process," Mary says with more conviction than she feels.

For the rest of the day, while she catches up on household chores, Mary can't shake the feeling of impending doom. Is it possible the Crawfords have enough power in this town to send her to prison for a crime she didn't commit?

When Jodi returns from making deliveries, her face is set in stone. "What happened?" Mary asks.

"I talked to my husband on the phone. According to Frank, Bob Crawford is notorious for bribing people with enormous sums of money to get what he wants. Building inspectors are at the top of the list, followed closely by politicians and law enforcement personnel."

"And Frank never mentioned this to you before?"

Jodi shakes her head. "He was covering for Bob. Frank feels guilty, and he's willing to testify on your behalf."

"No way, Jodi! I appreciate his concern, but I can't have anyone getting in trouble on account of me."

CHAPTER 10

Mary lies awake most of the night worrying about the possibility of a jail sentence. When she wakes to pouring rain on Sunday morning, she stays in bed all day with Biscuit curled up beside her.

Jodi calls early Monday morning to say she has an important errand to run and won't be in until after lunch. Mary spends the morning doing money chores and creating Angel Flowers. Between being arrested on Friday and yesterday's foul weather, she never made it to the grocery over the weekend, and when noon rolls around, with nothing in the house to eat, she orders takeout from the Crooked Porch. Despite the blazing heat, she walks over to the square to pick up her order. Her gut experiences a crushing blow at the sight of Jodi having lunch with Susan and several of her other former-life friends.

Mary leaves the Crooked Porch without picking up her order and hurries home. She remembers Jodi's words from Saturday. *Daisy will start running her mouth about framing you for theft. If I get her on tape, you're off the hook.* Jodi is playing with fire. And Mary won't be able to live with herself if something bad happens to Jodi. Returning to her past life is in Jodi's best interests. If Daisy and Bob Crawford have their way, Mary will soon go to prison. Which means Jodi will have no friends and no way to occupy her time.

Mary pulls herself together and is waiting in a rocker on the front porch when Jodi arrives forty-five minutes later. Mary gets up and stands at the top of the steps so Jodi can't pass.

"Our partnership isn't working out for me." Mary shoves a rolled-up bundle of cash at Jodi. "Here's what I owe you for last week, plus a little bonus."

Jodi's mouth falls open. "I don't understand. I thought everything was going well. We were making a difference, really helping people. Did I do something to upset you?"

Mary looks away, unable to endure the hurt in Jodi's kind brown eyes. Mary reminds herself she's doing Jodi a favor. She's better off in her former life. Besides, other than Daisy, those other women aren't so bad.

"I'm dismantling the business. It's too much to keep up with. I'm going to give the money to charity."

"But you still need someone to help collect and count. I'll do it for free. I don't need the income. Frank got the job at the lumberyard. He starts today. His salary is way higher than what Bob Crawford was paying him."

Jodi's urgent and pleading tone is a knife stabbing Mary in the heart. Her eyes meet Jodi's. She deserves the truth. "Your old friends have more to offer you than me."

Jodi studies Mary's face. "Is that what this is about? Did you see me having lunch at the Crooked Porch?"

Mary doesn't respond.

"I was trying to get some intel on Daisy about the charges she's pressing against *you*," Jodi says, her tone now bordering on angry.

"I figured as much." Curiosity gets the best of Mary. "Did you learn anything?"

"No. Their lips were sealed."

"I appreciate you trying." Mary inhales a deep breath. "Listen, Jodi, you're not doing yourself any favors by hanging out with the town pariah. If I don't go to prison, I'm moving to a new town to start a new life. Whoever buys this house will inherit the curse of the tree. Go back to your friends. Pretend you never met me."

Mary turns her back on Jodi and goes inside the house, closing the door and leaning against it. Ten minutes later, she's still standing there with tears streaming down her face when Phil knocks on the door.

"What's wrong, Mary? Did something else happen?"

His concern makes her cry harder. Through sobs, she says, "Jodi and I had a . . . a falling-out. She won't be helping me with the flowers anymore."

Phil scrunches up his face. "But the two of you seemed so close."

"We barely know each other. I'm carrying a lot of baggage. And she's too nice to be dragged down with me."

"I seriously doubt she sees it that way. Come here." He takes her in his arms. The scent of his woodsy cologne makes her knees go weak. She reminds herself he has a girlfriend, and Mary is going to prison.

She pushes him away. "You're obviously here for a reason. Did you learn something about my case?"

He gestures at the sofa. "Can we sit down?"

Mary furrows her brow. "More bad news?"

"It's neither good nor bad. It's just news."

"In that case . . ." She leads him to the sofa, and they sit down, side by side.

"The judge wants you to go for a psychiatric evaluation,"

Phil says. "Considering the situation with the tree, he feels it's important to prove you're of sound mind."

"Because the judge, along with everyone else in this town, thinks I'm crazy."

"Not me. I'm telling anyone who will listen that I've seen the money with my own eyes."

"I wouldn't do that if I were you. People might think you're crazy too."

"Let them." Phil grabs the box of tissues from the coffee table and holds it out to her.

Mary snatches a tissue and wipes her nose.

"Honestly, I think the psychiatric exam could help. People might take you more seriously if they know you're mentally stable. I can schedule the evaluation for you if you'd like."

She hangs her head. "Sounds like I don't have much choice. I'm done with this town. As soon as this court case is over, assuming I don't go to prison, I'm moving away to a town where no one knows me."

"But this is your home."

Her throat swells with the threat of more tears. "It hasn't felt like home since my parents died."

"Don't do anything rash, Mary. You've been through a lot these past weeks. Let things settle down before you make any major decisions. As for you going to prison, I don't think the district attorney has much of a case." Phil chuckles. "He wasn't pleased when I told him I have a witness who will testify that Daisy Crawford lost her diamond tennis bracelet."

Mary feels guilty for making Jodi testify after blowing her off just now. "Do you know which witnesses he's planning to call?"

"He gave me the list," Phil says. "Most of them are the building contractors you paid to fix up your house."

Mary thinks about all the nice men who worked on her

house. "I don't see how they can hurt me. The sum of the cash I paid them is way more than the amount Daisy claims I stole from her."

"That's an important point, Mary." Phil removes his phone from his pocket and creates a note to himself. "What will you do without Jodi? You can't manage your thriving business alone."

The burden of her responsibilities weighs heavily on Mary. She told Jodi she was quitting the Angel Flowers. But she isn't ready to do that just yet. "I'll figure something out."

"Maybe you should scale back your Angel Flower deliveries from seven days a week to three or four."

Mary considers his suggestion. "I can't do that. Too many people in our area are suffering. Besides, that would leave me with a surplus of money and flowers."

"Then I'll help you. I can come over every morning for a few hours before my shop opens at ten."

Mary shakes her head adamantly. "No way. You can't neglect your business like that. You're already working on my court case."

He stands to go. "I get to choose how I spend my time, Mary. And I'm not taking no for an answer. I'll see you in the morning."

True to his word, Phil is waiting on her front porch the following morning when Mary goes out for the newspaper. He hands her a to-go cup of coffee. "I brought you my special brew."

Mary looks down at the coffee and back up at him. "I'm not much of a coffee drinker."

Phil's blue eyes twinkle. "I think you'll like this. I order it especially from Guatemala."

Mary accepts the cup and takes a sip. Instead of being bitter, the black coffee is smooth and rich. "This is delicious. It would be better with cream and sugar."

Phil feigns indignation. "That would ruin the taste. I prefer to savor the coffee." He takes the newspaper from her. "You don't need to see this."

"Ugh! What now?" Mary snatches it back from him. Once again, she's front-page news. She scans the article, a piece by reporter Calvin Phelps, who outlines the pending court case brought by socialite Daisy Crawford against Crazy Mary, the town kook who claims money grows on her maple tree.

She folds the paper and tucks it under her arm. "Don't these reporters have anything better to write about?"

"Apparently not, I'm sorry to say. This is only the beginning of Daisy Crawford's smear campaign. Calvin is one of many in her back pocket."

And Phil is right. Articles about Crazy Mary appear in the paper at least every other day. Mary gets so tired of seeing her name in headlines, she cancels her subscription to the *Linden Falls Gazette*.

As the hot days of August wear on, Mary settles into her new routine. She pays Robbie, a teenage boy who lives down the street, to deliver the Angel Flowers. Robbie is so thrilled about the handsome sum she's paying in cash, he's more than willing to play dumb when asked who the flowers are from.

Phil arranges for Mary's psychiatric evaluation in the nearby town of Rutland. The psychiatrist is an attractive woman in her forties by the name of Shirley Chapman. Dr. Chapman's calm presence sets Mary at ease. The test is going well, and Mary suspects she's passing with flying colors, when the doctor quizzes her about her money tree. Mary has no choice but to tell the truth. And she gets the feeling Dr. Chapman doesn't believe her.

Phil brings Mary muffins and warm scones every

morning from Cobblestone Deli & Bakery. And Mary purchases a coffeemaker for him to brew his special Guatemalan coffee. After the yard work is complete, she makes breakfast for him—omelets and pancakes and French toast—before he heads to work at Bertie's Petals.

Phil's gentle manner makes him easy to talk to, and Mary opens up to him about her failed marriage. Phil, in turn, talks about his wife's illness and the struggles of managing her floral business. His expression and tone soften when he speaks of Lily. He's obviously crazy about her. Does Lily know about Mary? Would she object to Phil spending time with another woman? Mary reminds herself that she is his client. But whatever is developing between them feels like more.

Despite her time spent with Phil, Mary misses Jodi. She catches glimpses of Jodi around town. Filling up with gas. Leaving the library with a stack of books. Exiting the Corner Market with a bag of groceries. Much to Mary's surprise, Jodi is always alone.

On the third Thursday in August, Mary is taking Biscuit for his evening stroll when she senses someone following her. When she turns around, no one is there. But the eerie feeling of being watched persists. She's sure someone is peeking at her through the windows and spying on her while she's working in the yard. She's constantly on the lookout for suspicious people and cars. Which causes her to become increasingly on edge. Is she losing her mind? Maybe she really is going crazy.

She's in the grocery store two days later, scratching and sniffing cantaloupes, when she senses a presence behind her. She spins around to face Jodi. "Are you stalking me?"

Jodi appears taken aback. "Of course not. What makes you say that?"

Mary looks away. "Never mind."

"I just wanted to say hello, Mary. I miss you. As you suggested, I tried rekindling my relationship with my former friends. But I no longer fit in with their group. They're so negative about everything. It's despicable the way they talk behind one another's back. I don't know how I put up with them for all those years. I enjoy your company. Our friendship was meaningful. At least that's what I thought. Would you consider giving me another chance?"

Mary yearns to be friends with Jodi again. But for Jodi's sake, she must wait until her future is certain. "It's not you, Jodi. I'm a wreck right now with this court case coming up. I just need to figure a few things out."

"When is your hearing?"

"At the end of next week."

"I'll be thinking about you. I'm here if you need anything." Jodi embraces Mary, oblivious to the cantaloupe Mary is cradling in her arms.

Mary doesn't respond, for fear she might break into tears. She abandons the remaining items on her list and pushes her cart to the checkout. She's loading the bags in her truck when, once again, she senses someone watching her. She shakes off the feeling—she needs to get a grip—and speeds home.

On Sunday morning, she's in the yard raking money into piles when she hears a clicking noise. She looks around, expecting to see a squirrel gathering nuts. Instead, she spots a young woman with a camera straddling her fence.

CHAPTER 11

Mary drops her rake and races to the fence. "What're you doing? This is private property. You're trespassing." She grabs the girl's foot and yanks hard.

The girl kicks, trying to free her leg. "Wait! Stop! You're gonna make me fall. I'm not the enemy, Mary. I'm trying to help you."

Mary stops tugging at her leg, but she doesn't let go. "Help me how? And how do you know my name?"

"I'm Annie Mann, from *The Rutland Daily Times*. I'm researching your case. Please! If you let me get down, I'll explain."

This gets Mary's attention. Rutland, located forty-five minutes from Linden Falls, is one of the biggest cities in the state. *The Rutland Daily Times* is the biggest and oldest newspaper in the state. "All right," she says, letting out a sigh. "I'll give you five minutes."

Annie slings the camera strap over her shoulder and eases her way to the ground. "So, there's the infamous Money Maple."

Mary follows Annie across the yard, studying her while

she circles the tree, snapping photographs. She's a strikingly pretty girl, a wholesome beauty with long, curly blonde hair and crystal-blue eyes.

"This is truly remarkable," Annie says.

Mary folds her arms over her chest and taps her foot. "You just wasted a minute. You have four left. Start talking. Why are you interested in my case?"

Annie lowers her camera. "For starters, I needed to see the tree with my own eyes to believe it."

Mary sweeps an arm at the pile of cash. "But you can see it, right? Not everyone can."

"Yes! I can definitely see it. Wonder why others can't."

"That's the million-dollar question." Mary inclines her head at Annie's camera. "Does the money show up in the photos you took?"

Annie furrows her blonde brow. "I haven't checked." She presses buttons on the back of the camera. "You're right. I don't see any money, only dirt at the base of the tree. Look." She holds the camera's viewfinder up for Mary.

"I'm not surprised," Mary says. "We may never solve the mystery of why some can and some can't see the money. What's your other reason for being interested in my case?"

"I've been following your story since it first broke. I think you're getting a bum deal. I think Daisy Crawford's setting you up, and I aim to prove it."

Mary narrows her eyes. "Why? What's in it for you?"

"If you're familiar with our paper, you know our reach is broad. We have a number of subscribers in Linden Falls."

"I'm familiar with the *Daily Times*."

"We've heard from several subscribers about mysterious gifts of flowers and cash being sent anonymously to sick people and those who are down on their luck. We received a tip that the person sending those mysterious gifts is you. I've been following you and your delivery boy these past few days. And I'm convinced you're the Flower Angel. You're doing a good thing, Mary. Why do you wish to remain anonymous?"

"I have my reasons." Mary wipes sweat off her brow. "Woo-wee, it's gonna be a scorcher. I realize it's early, but I could use some iced tea. Would you like some?"

"Sure," Annie says, and they walk together to the house.

Seated at the farm table with glasses of tea in front of them, Mary attempts to explain what led her to make certain choices. "It was like winning the lottery at first. I used some of the money to fix up my house. And I bought a new wardrobe and a luxury SUV to fulfill some misguided notion Daisy would accept me as a friend if I owned the same material goods as she. Of course, that backfired. Daisy pressed charges, and things went south from there. The money became a burden. There's so much of it. I ran out of places to hide it." She tells Annie about the second wish and the ensuing storm. "Then I realized. The money isn't meant for me. I'm simply the catalyst."

"But telling the truth would clear your name. When people find out you're behind the gifts, they'll believe you about the money tree."

Mary hangs her head, staring down at the table. "I'm not so sure about that. Everyone in this town seems to have it in for me. They call me Crazy Mary. My attorney is confident we'll win the court case. When I do, I'm planning to sell this house and move to a new town. Whoever buys the place will have to deal with the curse of the tree."

"I don't blame you for being bitter. But you seem like a good person, and I'd like to help you." Annie pauses a beat. "My friend Molly is an investigative reporter at the NBC affiliate station in Rutland. I'm sure she'd be interested in sharing your story. Between the two of us, we could get the truth out to the folks of Linden Falls."

CAREFUL WHAT YOU WISH

Mary looks up at the young woman. Annie's excitement is infectious. But Mary doesn't have much faith in the folks of Linden Falls. "I'll have to think about it."

"Think fast. We're pressed for time with your court case coming up at the end of the week." Annie looks at her watch. "I should be going. My five minutes were up a half hour ago."

She stands and walks her empty glass to the sink. "Thank you for your time, Mary. I understand this isn't easy for you. But your story's human-interest angle is huge. Our world is full of so much anger and greed these days. A generous spirit like yours should be celebrated."

"That's kind of you to say. Thank you, Annie." Mary motions her toward the hallway. "I'll show you to the door. Unless you prefer to climb back over the fence."

Annie burst out laughing. "I've had enough fence climbing for one day." At the front door, she hands Mary a business card with her numbers. "I'm staying at the Wishing Tree Inn. Let me know if you have questions or want to talk more. I hope to hear from you soon."

FOR THE REST of the day on Sunday, Mary stews over what to do about Annie's offer. Finally, late afternoon, she texts Phil, explaining she has a situation relating to her case and asking if he's available for a brief meeting. He responds immediately. *Doc's Fountain in ten minutes?*

On my way, she texts back.

Phil is seated at a table by the window when she arrives. "After spending the afternoon going over books at the flower shop, I'm rewarding myself with a maple creemee. Can I tempt you with one?"

The mention of maple creemees brings back memories

from childhood. "I don't know when I last had a maple creemee. But I don't need the calories."

"Life is short, Mary. You should indulge in simple pleasures more often." He flashes his deliciously mischievous grin. If only he didn't have a girlfriend and Mary's life wasn't a red-hot mess.

Mary's mouth waters thinking about the delicious treat. "In that case, how can I resist?"

Phil waves the waitress over and orders two maple creemees. He waits for the waitress to leave before asking, "What's going on? Did something happen?"

Mary tells him about her encounter with Annie. "I'm torn. Should I let her tell my story? I'm a private person. I don't want my laundry aired over the news and in all the papers."

"Last I checked, your laundry is already being aired in the papers." He tilts his head to the side, giving her an adorable expression, a mixture between sweet and sassy. This man is really getting to her. The sooner she can win her court case and leave town the better.

"While that may be true, I'm not sure I want the whole town knowing I'm the Flower Angel."

Phil folds his hands on the table. "What purpose does keeping it a secret serve?"

"This may sound silly, but I have a hunch the tree wants me to remain anonymous."

"The tree doesn't have a brain or feelings, Mary."

Mary's face warms. "I know. I told you it was silly."

The waitress delivers their maple creemees. "Enjoy," she says, slapping the bill face-down on the table beside Phil.

Mary drags her tongue up the soft serve ice cream, savoring the sweetness. "Oh, my! This is better than I remember."

"See? I told you." Phil takes several licks before his face

CAREFUL WHAT YOU WISH

grows serious. "I was going to wait and share this news tomorrow. But since the weekend is almost over, you might as well know. I got a call late in the day on Friday. The psychiatrist, Shirley Chapman, is asking the judge to have you committed to the Vermont State Asylum for further evaluation. She says your tree hallucinations may be a symptom of schizophrenia."

"I am not schizophrenic." Mary brings her fist crashing down on the table, causing patrons at nearby tables to stare at her. "You've seen the money too, Phil. You rake it up every morning. If I'm schizo, then so are you."

"Neither of us is mentally insane, Mary. If I could share this burden with you, I would. Unfortunately, you're the one being charged with grand larceny."

"Why do you think some people can see the money and others can't?"

"I wish I knew," Phil says as he bites into his waffle cone.

"It's the strangest thing. Annie admitted she could see the cash. But the money didn't show up in the pictures she took. I can't shake the feeling the tree is trying to tell me something." Her hand shoots up, palm out. "I know. Don't say it. The tree isn't human." She points at the ceiling. "But somebody up there is sending me a message."

"Hence the reason they call you the Flower Angel." He smiles and stuffs the rest of his cone in his mouth.

"Maybe the message isn't just for me. Maybe the message is meant for everyone in Linden Falls." She holds her cone out to him. "Do you want the rest? I can't eat any more."

He takes the cone. "It will spoil my dinner, but why not? YOLO, as Lily says."

Lily again. Why does Phil's girlfriend creep into all their conversations?

"Do you trust this journalist?" Phil asks.

Mary thinks before she answers. "I probably shouldn't.

It's hard to know who in the media you can trust these days. But I do. She's young and enthusiastic. And she seems to genuinely care."

"How many arrangements have you given away to date?"

"Gosh. I don't know for sure." Mary reaches for a napkin and wipes her mouth. "Hundreds."

"Wow. That's a lot of people you've helped, not only by sending beautiful flowers to brighten their days but giving them cold hard cash to help them during hard times. I can only imagine how grateful some of these people might feel. Why don't you ask the journalists to share some of these stories? It certainly won't hurt your case. And it might endear the townsfolk to you."

Mary balls up her napkin and drops it on the table. "When does the judge have in mind to commit me to the asylum?"

"I assume he'll announce it when he hears your case in court on Friday." Phil reaches for her hand. "Don't worry. We'll figure something out. I won't let them lock you up."

Mary's gut hardens, and she worries she might vomit up her maple creemee. Despite his best intentions, Phil won't be able to save her if the judge sends her to the loony bin.

CHAPTER 12

Mary arranges a lunch meeting with Annie and Molly for noon on Monday at the Crooked Porch Café. Molly is as glamorous as Annie is the girl next door. But her smile is genuine, her tone sincere.

Mary's mouth falls open when the young women order bacon cheeseburgers. She wags her finger at them. "You'd better enjoy that youthful metabolism while it lasts."

Annie laughs. "I rarely eat hamburgers. But rumor has it these are the best in the state."

"It's true what they say about the camera adding ten pounds," Molly adds. "The additional calories mean an extra thirty minutes in the gym tonight."

"That sounds like torture." Mary studies the menu. "I think I'll stick with the grilled chicken breast and side salad."

Molly gives her the once-over. "What're you worried about, Mary? You have an adorable figure."

Mary forces a smile. Adorable means rail thin with no curves and bumps instead of hills.

"So, Mary." Annie removes her iPad from her work tote bag and places it on the table. "Molly and I have been brainstorming all morning. As I mentioned yesterday, we'll be simultaneously launching your news story. We have some exciting ideas about different angles of approach. We'd love your input. Or, if you prefer, we can surprise you."

Mary straightens in her chair. "You girls know best how to do your jobs. But there's one thing I want to make clear. This story is make or break for me," she says and tells them about the psychiatric evaluation and the judge threatening to send her to Vermont State Asylum.

Annie rolls her eyes. "That's ridiculous. I've seen the Maple Money with my own eyes."

"So have several other people," Mary says.

Annie and Molly exchange a look Mary can't interpret. "I think you'll be pleased with what we have planned," Annie says.

"Keep in mind, I'm running out of time. My case goes to court on Friday."

"Don't worry," Molly says. "Your story is top priority."

The waitress brings their drinks, freshly squeezed limeades for everyone. They place their orders, and the waitress leaves.

Molly takes a sip of limeade and sets down her glass. "We'd like to interview you, Mary."

Mary gulps back a wave of fear. "You mean on TV?"

"It won't be live. We'll record the interview in advance." Molly smiles warmly at her. You'll do great, Mary. The audience will love you. Our program manager is so excited about your story, he's allotting us a full thirty minutes. This will be a trial run for my own show—*A Special Report with Molly Chandler.*"

Annie winks at Mary. "Molly is the most driven person I know. This is a big opportunity for her, and she won't mess it up. Molly will ask the questions, but I'll be there as well. I'll adapt the interview for my feature in the paper."

CAREFUL WHAT YOU WISH

"I promise we'll keep it informal," Molly says.

Annie nods her head. "We'll set up in your kitchen. If you've never seen Molly in action, she's a real pro. You'll never even know the camera is in the room."

"The show will air at five thirty on Wednesday. And Annie's feature will appear in Thursday morning's paper." Molly talks as she fingers the screen on her iPad. "We have a full day of interviews already scheduled for tomorrow. We'll tape your segment first thing on Wednesday morning if that works for you."

Mary shakes her head. "Mornings aren't good for me. That's when I collect the money and arrange the Angel Flowers. Can't it wait until the afternoon, after the deliveries go out?"

Annie rests a hand on Mary's shoulder. "You're missing the point. Our viewers want to see you in action, the love and compassion you put into the Angel Flowers."

Mary was afraid of this. The story, once it airs, will blow her cover. The tree might even stop producing. Although that would be a good thing. She could do without the headache of collecting and counting the money. For Mary, the satisfaction comes from identifying the donees and delivering the Angel Flowers in secret. Helping people has kept Mary's head above water these past few weeks. She never stopped to think that some of these same people, her donees, called her Crazy Mary for believing money grows on trees.

THE TOWN BUZZES with activity as Molly and Annie, accompanied by Molly's camera crews and Annie's photographers, interview folks on Main Street and in the square. Mary is not privy to what transpires during these discussions, but she senses the improvement in the overall mood of the townsfolk. Everyone is cheerful, and there's an air of conspiracy, as though they're all in on a great big secret.

Mary's upcoming interview is at the forefront of her mind. She makes pages of notes on a legal pad. If she says the wrong thing, she could come across as mentally unstable. *Crazy Mary.*

Annie texts on Tuesday night to inform Mary the team will arrive at six o'clock on Wednesday morning.

Mary awakens in plenty of time to style her hair and smear on a little makeup. She dresses simply in a crisp white sleeveless blouse and designer blue jeans. When the doorbell rings, she greets an onslaught of men and women loaded down with equipment—video cameras and microphones. One poor fella is carrying a wide-screen television that's bigger than him.

Annie and Molly bring up the rear. Annie is a ray of sunshine in a yellow floral sundress, while Molly is dressed more professionally in a navy pantsuit and cream-colored silk blouse.

"What's the TV for?" Mary asks.

"It's a surprise," Annie answers.

When concern crosses Mary's face, Molly puts an arm around Mary, pulling her in for a half hug. "You have nothing to worry about, Mary. We will cut out any awkward moments, and you get to sign off on the final version before airing."

Mary sucks in an unsteady breath. "Okay then. Let's get this thing over."

"Don't think of it as a burden," Molly says. "Relax, I promise you'll have fun."

The camera crew swarms her kitchen, rearranging the furniture to make room for their equipment. They position the wide-screen television behind the armchairs where Mary and Molly will sit. A female crew member with a crop of gray curls attaches a microphone to Mary's blouse and announces, "Show time!"

"I'm Molly Chandler, joining you this evening from Linden Falls. I have the pleasure of interviewing Mary Ellis May. Most of you are aware of Linden Falls' famous Wishing Tree. I imagine many of you have even visited the tree and pinned your own wishes to its branches with satin ribbon. Mary's wish brought her good fortune, which she has generously shared with many sick and troubled citizens of her hometown." Molly angles her body toward Mary. "Tell us about your wish, Mary."

Panic temporarily renders Mary paralyzed. Remembering what's at stake, she tunes out the cameras and focuses her attention on Molly. "I made the wish on a whim. I'd lost my job, and I was about to lose my home. I wished money would grow on trees. I imagine everyone has wished that sometime in their lives. Of course, I didn't expect it to come true, but next thing I know, money is dropping from the maple tree in my backyard.

"I went on a spending spree, but I quickly ran out of things to buy. When word about the tree got out, my neighbors and friends didn't believe me. The local paper referred to me as Crazy Mary. Everyone laughed at me behind my back. I tied a second wish to the tree, asking for the tree to stop producing money. That night, there was a terrible storm, and the next morning, there was more money than ever covering my yard.

"That's when I knew I was meant to do something meaningful with the money. I began identifying the citizens of Linden Falls who need financial aid. And I sent them anonymous donations along with arrangements of flowers."

Molly holds up one of Mary's Invisible Garden cards. "The giver of these gifts from the Invisible Garden soon became known around town as the Flower Angel. We'll hear from some of those special people now. Roll tape."

The television flashes on behind them, and an attractive woman in her thirties appears. She tells the story of her young child with a rare blood disorder. "The donation allowed us to see a specialist." Tears stream down the woman's face. "Thanks to the Flower Angel, my daughter is finally getting the help she needs."

Next up is a man with seven children who lost his job and his wife. "The money came at a crucial time, when I was about to lose my home. Thanks to the Flower Angel, I have a new job. My kids and I are seeing a grief counselor, and our lives are back on track."

A young mother holding a tiny baby is last. "I was homeless and about to give birth. I now have an apartment, childcare for my baby, and a new job."

The screen goes dark, and Molly says to Mary, "Your generosity has helped so many. How does that make you feel?"

Mary pauses a beat to compose herself. "I am humbled by their stories. When this whole thing started, I was looking for happiness in all the wrong places. Thanks to the tree, I now realize that our health and the well-being of our loved ones are all that really matters."

"So, Mary . . ." Molly repositions herself as she changes the subject. "I understand not everyone can see the money when it falls from the tree. Why do you think that is?"

Mary lets out a small sigh. "I've been thinking a lot about that lately, and I've come to the only plausible conclusion. When you hold the money in your hand, it's just money, currency you used to pay for goods and services. But to witness it fall from the tree is magic. And to experience that magic, you must believe in miracles. You have to be willing to open your heart to the possibility of a being greater than us." She shifts her gaze heavenward.

"Like a divine intervention?" Molly asks.

Mary nods. "Like a divine intervention."

Molly looks into the camera. "We've learned a lot from speaking with your donation recipients. It astounded them to learn their money came from Crazy Mary's maple tree. They feel guilty for not believing in you. And they wanted to thank you in person." She gestures at the window, where dozens of people are gathered at the base of the tree in her backyard.

Mary gets up and goes out to the porch. When they see her, the crowd cheers and waves. Mary recognizes some faces from the testimonial video. Jodi and Phil are front and center. A teenager stands close to Phil. She looks oddly familiar. Is she a donee? When the crowd chants her name, Mary walks out to the yard and wades through the sea of flowers to the tree.

Annie and Molly appear beside Mary as a second camera crew records the scene. The young mother from the video, her baby cradled in her arms, steps forward. "They have nominated me as spokesperson. On behalf of this group, thank you from the bottom of our hearts for taking interest in our problems. We also want to ask your forgiveness for doubting you about the money tree. You've taught us a lot, Flower Angel. We'll never forget you, and we'll always be grateful."

Mary no longer tries to hide her tears. "It's *I* who should be thanking *you*. You have restored my faith in humankind. We all make poor decisions based on greed and envy and all the many sins that drag us down. But God created us as equals. Innocent and pure and good. We owe it to Him to emanate that goodness as much as possible."

Molly orders the camera crew to stop taping. She places

an arm around Mary's shoulders. "Because of you, these wonderful people are believers."

As if on cue, the crowd leans over and grabs handfuls of paper bills, tossing them in the air. Mary crosses her hands over her heart. *They can see it.*

Mary waits until everyone settles down. "Thank you all for coming today, and for your testimonials. You mean the world to me. In an organized manner, I want everyone to collect the cash around them, your final gift from the tree."

After peacefully and respectfully gathering their share of money, with tears of joy, each member of the group offers Mary a hug of gratitude in parting.

Annie waves Jodi over. "I'm going to rat on Jodi. I can't keep it a secret any longer. Jodi was the whistleblower. She made the anonymous tip that alerted us to your story."

A flush creeps up Jodi's neck to her cheeks. "I hope you're not mad, Mary. I had to do something. I love you so much, and I couldn't stand to see you go to prison for a crime you didn't commit." She gestures at the dispersing crowd. "All the good you've done for our community deserves to be celebrated."

"How could I possibly be mad?" Taking Jodi in her arms, Mary whispers, "I've missed you. And I love you, too."

Phil and the teenager approach. The girl's lips part in a smile that reaches her twinkling blue eyes, and everything suddenly makes sense. Lily isn't Phil's girlfriend. She's his daughter.

CHAPTER 13

When Phil makes the introductions, Mary holds out her hand to his daughter. "It's very nice to meet you, Lily."

"Same. I've heard a lot about you from my dad." Lily presents Mary with a pastry box. "I brought you some warm blueberry scones from Carly's Creations at the inn."

Mary takes the box. "My favorite. That's awfully kind of you." She sniffs the box. "These smell delicious. And I'm starving. Let's go inside and make some coffee."

The small entourage leaves the yard for the kitchen, where the camera crew is making a hasty departure.

"We need to head out," Annie says.

Mary appears disappointed. "Can't you stay for breakfast?"

Annie shakes her head. "Sorry, but we need to start editing this footage if we wanna make our noon deadline. I'll bring the final version over in a while for your approval."

"That's not necessary," Mary says. "I'm thrilled with the interview, and I trust you to make the appropriate edits. I'd rather watch it on TV, anyway."

Annie locks eyes with Molly. "In that case, let's get to it."

Mary walks Annie and Molly to the front door. "I can't thank the two of you enough. You are the angels, not me. You may very well have saved me from a prison sentence."

Molly flashes her kilowatt smile. "The camera loves you, Mary. You came across as being honest and sincere. You've already touched so many lives. Your story is about to touch millions more."

"I fully expect this story to go viral," Annie says. "The judge will be hard-pressed to convict the town's most famous benefactress."

Mary's face warms. "I hope you're right." She gives each of them a hug and closes the door behind them.

She returns to the kitchen to find Jodi and Lily standing at the back door, having an in-depth discussion about the flower types in Mary's yard. Lily has one hand on Biscuit's head, absently rubbing his ears.

"She's a lovely girl," Mary says to Phil, who is counting scoops of coffee as he dumps them into the coffeemaker.

His lips part in a soft smile. "Thank you. She's a lot like her mom. She's gotten me through the worst of days."

"She knows an awful lot about flowers for someone so young."

"From the time she was a little girl, she loved hanging out with Alice at the shop." Phil snickers. "My wife wanted to name her Iris. I thought it was too old-fashioned. We settled on Lily."

"The name suits her."

"I should've put her to work at the shop sooner," Phil says. "She's proven to be an asset, not only in processing orders but in creating arrangements as well. She'll be a senior in high school next year. She's hoping to attend a college with a strong horticulture program."

"Good for her." Moseying over to the back door, Mary

leans into Lily. "I'm taking the day off, and I'd hate for the flowers to go to waste. Would you like to cut some for the shop?"

Lily's face brightens. "I'd love that." She looks over at Phil for approval. "Is that okay, Dad?"

"Of course, sweetheart. You'll find clippers and buckets in the garden shed. I'll be out to help you in a minute."

Lily hurries outside with Biscuit trotting along beside her.

Phil announces, "Coffee's ready, ladies."

Jodi and Mary turn away from the back door. As they are doctoring their coffees with cream and sugar, Mary says, "I'm in the mood to celebrate, and I have a hankering for my grandmother's chicken potpie. Her recipe is the best I've ever tasted. I haven't made it in years. Please say you'll both come for dinner. Bring Lily and Frank with you and get here in time to watch Molly's program at five thirty."

"Lily is going to the movies with friends," Phil says. "But I would love to come. I'll bring the libations. I make a mean cucumber martini."

"I'm only coming if I can help prepare dinner," Jodi says.

Mary loops her arm through Jodi's. "Offer accepted. Now that we're friends again, I'm not letting you go. We'll shop for groceries first and then spend the afternoon together in the kitchen."

"This sounds like my cue to leave," Phil says, filling a to-go cup with coffee. "If I don't supervise my daughter, she's liable to cut every stem."

"She can have them all," Mary says, waving him on. "Just leave us a handful for the table."

Once he's gone, Mary and Jodi sit down at the table with their coffees and blueberry scones. "I don't know how I'll ever repay you for what you did for me today," Mary says.

"You owe me nothing," Jodi says, pinching off a bite of scone. "Your story deserved to be told."

Mary stares down at her coffee. "I'm sorry for the way I treated you. I didn't want you and Frank getting into trouble because of me."

"No way was I going to sit by and watch you go to jail. You and I have both been burned by women claiming to be our friends. I wanted to prove to you I'm not that kind of woman. You can count on me. Whether or not you like it, I'm your friend for keeps."

A tear spills from Mary's eyelid and slides down her cheek. "You do not know how much that means to me."

JODI AND MARY remain at the kitchen table for hours, rehashing the events of the morning and preparing their grocery list for dinner. On the way to the market, they stop in at the Crooked Porch Café for lunch. As luck would have it, some of Daisy's friends are seated beside them. The women talk ugly about Mary and Jodi, loud enough for them to hear.

Mary laughs at them. "I can't believe I once cared what those women think of me."

A sorrowful expression crosses Jodi's face. "I can't believe I was once one of them."

Mary smiles at her. "That was in the past. We have each other now."

Jodi smiles back. "I would rather have one genuine friend like you than a dozen fake friends like them."

Mary and Jodi spend the afternoon in the kitchen, rolling out homemade dough crusts for the potpie and making the cake for strawberry shortcake, another one of Mary's grandmother's recipes.

"Did your grandmother have any special recipes?" Mary asks Jodi.

"Yes! Cheese straws. In fact, I've been perfecting the recipe during my spare time these past couple of weeks. I'm thinking of marketing them."

"That's a great idea. I've figured out the key to marketing. We can sell anything if we find the right packaging, come up with a catchy name, and create a cute label."

Once the pie is assembled, while the cake is in the oven, Jodi prepares a melon and prosciutto salad, and Mary mixes up batter for corn bread. They set the table on the back screened porch with a pink-gingham tablecloth, bouquet of wildflowers from the garden, and Mary's grandmother's floral china.

Jodi goes home to change around four. Mary dresses in a blue sleeveless sheath and fastens her hair back in a low ponytail with tendrils around her face and her mama's pearl teardrop earrings in her ears.

Phil arrives promptly at five with a cooler and reusable grocery bag. While Mary removes the ingredients for her charcuterie board from the refrigerator, Phil unloads the contents of his bag onto the counter. A plastic container of seeded cucumber. A bottle each of Effen cucumber vodka and vermouth. A cocktail shaker and four martini glasses.

They work side by side in companionable silence as though they've prepared cocktails and appetizers together many times before. Phil adds several jigger glasses of Effen cucumber vodka to his concoction, puts the top on the shaker, and gives it a good shake. He pours the green liquid into two martini glasses, handing one to Mary.

Turning around to face the room, he lets out a contented sigh. "If I lived here, I'd spend all my time in the kitchen. I can almost sense the presence of friendly ghosts, your family members who lived here in decades past."

Martini in hand, Mary turns her back to the counter. "I'm going to have to renovate, sooner rather than later. My oven is on its last leg. I hope it doesn't give out on me tonight while the pie is baking." Mary gestures at the armchairs. "And I need to replace those. The back leg on one is broken. I was terrified it would topple over and dump Molly on the floor this morning. My goal is to keep the decor simple, hoping to recreate the same vibe."

"Does this mean you're staying in Linden Falls?" Phil asks.

"If I don't go to prison. Speaking of which, have you heard from Chief Norton?"

"Not yet. I don't expect to until after Molly's show airs." Phil turns toward Mary. "Don't worry if Daisy doesn't drop the charges. Our case is strong. We *will* win."

"What about the judge's threat to commit me to the Vermont State Asylum?"

"Considering the day's events, I'm pretty sure that's off the table."

"I hope you're right." Mary leans back against the counter. "I enjoyed meeting Lily. She seems like a sweet girl. I have a confession to make."

"What's that?" Phil asks as he sips his martini.

"When you talked about Lily before, I thought she was your girlfriend."

Phil lets out a belly laugh. "I haven't so much as looked at another woman since my wife died. Until now. I have feelings for you, Mary. More than the friendly kind of feelings. And they scare the hell out of me. But I can no longer deny them. Is there any chance you feel the same about me?"

A smile creeps on her lips. "I've been fighting them, because I thought you were already involved in a relationship. I admit I was pleased to find out Lily is your daughter." She sets her glass on the counter. "I'm scared, too, Phil. I've only been with one man in my life. I trusted him, and he betrayed me."

Taking her by the shoulders, he looks down at her, his beautiful deep blue eyes boring into her soul. "I would never do that to you."

He's a full head taller, and when she tears her gaze away from his eyes, she's looking at his chest. "We should wait. It wouldn't be fair to either of us to start anything until we settle my court case."

He tilts her chin toward him. "Extreme worst-case scenario, you're convicted and sentenced to one year. You'll get off on probation in six months. I'm not going anywhere, Mary. I'll be right here waiting for you."

He leans into her. He's going to kiss her, and she's going to let him, when Jodi and Frank burst into the kitchen.

CHAPTER 14

Phil and Mary jump apart. But their embarrassed faces give them away. Jodi's lip curls in a smirk. She knows Phil was about to kiss Mary.

Jodi's husband is a giant teddy bear of a man, an ex-linebacker in college. "Come here, girl." He engulfs Mary in a hug, lifting her off her feet. "I've heard so much about you. I'm thrilled to finally meet you."

"I'm glad to meet you as well," Mary says when he sets her down.

Jodi thrusts a plastic storage bag at Mary. "Here, I brought you some of the cheese straws I was telling you about."

Mary removes a cheese straw from the bag and takes a bite. The cheese is savory and the texture light and crispy. "These are delicious," she says with her mouth full. "You should totally market them."

"Maybe we should consider opening a booth at the farmers' market. We can sell your potpourri and special blended teas and my cheese straws."

"That's something to think about." While Mary loves the

CAREFUL WHAT YOU WISH

idea of going into business with Jodi, she can't make plans until her future is certain.

Jodi clicks on the television. "It's almost show time."

Mary takes the remote control from her. "Let's watch in the living room. This TV is so old the picture is fuzzy."

Jodi grabs the remote back. "It's cozier in here."

"I was saying the same thing right before you arrived," Phil says as he mixes another batch of martinis for Jodi and Frank.

Jodi whispers to Mary, "Looked to me like he was getting ready to kiss you right before we arrived."

Mary digs her elbow into Jodi's side. "Hush!"

Phil hands out drinks, and Mary places her charcuterie board on the farm table. "Everybody, dig in."

They stand around the television sipping and nibbling as they wait for the show to begin.

Molly appears on the screen. She's wearing a red dress and is seated behind a sleek desk. "Good evening. I'm Molly Chandler, and I have the privilege of bringing you a special report from Linden Falls, Vermont. The subject of our broadcast this evening is a remarkable woman whose story will warm your heart."

Molly speaks with dozens of donation recipients. Some say only a few words about their hard times while others go into detail about how significantly the donations altered their lives. Mary's interview takes up a chunk of time in the middle, followed by the scene in the yard with the donees. Mary reaches for the tissue box more than once during the thirty-minute show.

When the program ends, Phil turns off the television. "Mary, you're truly a miracle."

Mary blushes. "I can't take all the credit. I was following the tree's lead."

Frank coughs into his hand. "I'm feeling a little left out. Do I get to see this tree?" he says, and they all laugh.

Mary opens the back door, and they file out with Biscuit bringing up the rear.

Mary is walking on air as they wander around the backyard. Regardless of what happens with her court case, she feels vindicated. She is no longer the town pariah.

They share a pleasant dinner on the porch with candles flickering, crickets chirping in the background, and the ceiling fan rotating slowly overhead. The floral-scented air carries the promise of romance. Is it possible for Mary to find love again? Phil is handsome and successful and fun to be with. He's an honorable man. Can Mary live up to his standards?

While they eat, they talk about the upcoming change in seasons—football, cooler weather, and the droves of tourists who will flock to the state in search of fall foliage.

Everyone devours the meal, and the men go back for seconds. When they return to the table, Frank asks, "What's up next for you, Mary?"

"That depends on the outcome of my court case."

"I have faith you'll be exonerated," Frank says. "What then? Will you continue with the Angel Flowers?"

Mary sets down her fork and dabs her lips with her napkin. "That depends on the tree. I have a hunch my journey with the Money Maple may be nearing its end. If that's the case, I'll use a small amount of the money I have stashed away to renovate my kitchen, and I'll invest the rest. I'm thinking of starting a foundation that grants gifts to townsfolk in need." She pushes back from the table. "Time for dessert."

"I'll help you," Phil says, jumping to his feet and gathering up the dirty plates.

They're assembling the strawberry shortcake when the

front doorbell rings.

"I'll get it," Phil says, wiping his hands on a dish towel. He leaves the kitchen and a minute later he calls out, "Mary! Chief Norton is here to see you."

Mary squeezes her eyes shut, saying a silent prayer before joining Phil at the front door.

The chief tips his hat to her. "Evening, Mary. Sorry to interrupt your evening, but I thought you might want to know Daisy Crawford is dropping the charges against you."

Mary keeps a straight face despite her fluttering heart. "You don't say. Why so suddenly?"

The chief mops the sweat off his face with a bandana. "Daisy found her tennis bracelet when she was cleaning out her car. She feels just awful about accusing you of stealing it."

"I bet she does. What about the money? Did she find it too?"

"Well . . ." He stuffs the bandana back in his pocket. "She can't say for certain how much money she had in the safe."

Mary lets out a grunt. "She didn't have *any* money in the safe."

"Your word against hers will be difficult to prove in a court of law." The chief smiles at her. "This is good news, Mary May. Try to put this unpleasantness behind you and move on with your life."

"I plan to move on with my life, Chief. But I won't easily forget the night I spent in jail."

Phil places a hand on Mary's shoulder. "Let's be real here, Chief. We all know Molly Chandler's news show is the reason for Daisy's sudden change of heart. I have a message for Daisy Crawford, and I'd appreciate it if you'd deliver it to her. Tell her I'm advising my client to sue Daisy for defamation of character."

The chief's smile fades. "Now, Phil. Is that really necessary?"

"We think so," Phil says, and closes the door in the chief's face.

Mary claps a hand over her mouth and drags Phil by the arm back to the kitchen. They burst into laughter, as she gives him a high five. "Are we really going to sue her?"

"Not unless you want to. I don't think we have much of a case. But we'll have fun watching Daisy squirm for a while."

Mary pauses a beat, imagining Daisy's fall from grace. "I would love nothing more than to watch her squirm. But Chief Norton is right. It's time for me to put all this unpleasantness behind me." She grabs two dessert plates. "I can't wait to tell Jodi I've been exonerated."

Phil follows Mary out to the porch with the other two dessert plates. He places his plates in front of Jodi and Frank. "Looks like we forgot dessert forks. I'll get them," he says, turning back toward the kitchen.

"You won't believe this," Mary says, reclaiming her vacated chair. "Chief Norton just stopped by to tell me Daisy is dropping the charges.

Frank punches the air, and Jodi rolls her eyes. "Are you surprised?"

"She claims she found her diamond tennis bracelet when she was cleaning out her car," Mary says.

"That may be true," Jodi says. "But I wonder how long ago she found it."

"Whatever," Mary says. "It's over."

Phil returns with a bottle of champagne and four flutes. "This is cause for a celebration."

Mary smiles up at him. "So that's what was in the cooler. I admire your positive thinking."

"Never hurts to be prepared." Phil pops the cork and fills the flutes with golden liquid.

Several rounds of celebratory toasts ensue. The bubbly tickles Mary's nose and makes her feel giddy.

Phil refills the glasses. "I have an announcement to make. I'm returning to my law practice. Helping Mary with her case reminded me of how much I love the law."

Mary lifts her glass. "Congratulations. You're a fine attorney. Linden Falls needs someone with your integrity."

Phil sips his champagne. "I'm a better attorney than I am a florist for sure. My daughter, if she returns to Linden Falls after college, will take over the shop. In the meantime, I need to find someone . . . or someones . . . to run it for me. Mary, Jodi, would the two of you consider managing the business for me? The shop would give you a home base from which to sell your cheese straws and potpourri and whatever else you creative geniuses come up with."

Smiles spread across Mary's and Jodi's faces. "I'm game," Jodi says, and Mary adds, "Me too!"

Phil falls back in his chair. "Whew. That's a relief."

Jodi holds out her empty glass to Phil. With slurred words, she says, "Give me a refill. This is definitely something to celebrate."

Frank takes the glass from her. "You've had enough. Let's help Mary clean up, and then I'm taking you home."

Mary dismisses them with a wave. "You two go on. I've got this."

From across the table, Phil winks at Mary. "Correction. *We've* got this."

Jodi smacks her husband's arm. "Hear that, Frank? The lovebirds wanna be alone."

"Okay. That's it. Let's go home." Frank helps his wife to her feet, and when Mary rises from her chair to show them to the door, he says, "Don't get up. We can see ourselves out."

Lowering herself back to the chair, Mary waits for Frank and Jodi to leave the porch. "Are you sure about us managing the shop? I won't hold you to it if you change your mind tomorrow."

Phil chuckles. "We should probably confirm with Jodi tomorrow, to make sure she remembers. But I have no intention of changing my mind. I've been thinking about this for some time. Can you handle Bertie's Petals and Angel Flowers?"

"I'll figure something out." Mary gets up from the table. "I need to take Biscuit for his evening walk. Would you care to join me?"

"Sure. But let's clean up first."

After clearing the table and rinsing the dishes, Mary locates Biscuit's leash, and they head out toward the square. When they reach the corner, Mary asks, "What was your wife like?"

Phil hesitates before answering. "Alice was full of life. A regular little social butterfly, flittering from one event to another."

Mary experiences a pang of envy. "I've always admired women like that. I don't possess any social grace whatsoever."

"Your grace manifests itself differently, Mary. Your beauty shines from within. You're much easier to be around than Alice. She was extremely high-strung. You're a calming influence. And you're unpretentious. What you see is what you get. And I find that refreshing."

"That's nice of you to say. Thank you."

They walk the rest of the way in silence. When they get to the square, Mary leads them over to the Wishing Tree. She removes an envelope with her Invisible Garden logo from her pocket and attaches it to the Wishing Tree with a thin satin ribbon.

"Another wish?" Phil asks.

"Something like that." She's grateful when he doesn't press her for details.

Inside the envelope is a handwritten note thanking the tree for teaching her valuable lessons about friendship, helping others less fortunate, having faith in herself, and summoning the courage to start anew. She has a wish, but instead of pinning it on the tree, she'll keep it in her heart. She wishes for her tree to stop making money, to trust Mary to continue the work they started together. And to help some other poor lost soul find their way.

As they turn toward home, Phil takes the leash from her, and she loops her arm through his, resting her head on his shoulder.

They arrive home to find envelopes in a variety of sizes littering her porch.

"What're these?" Mary asks, bending down to pick up an envelope. She tears it open and removes a notecard. "It's from my neighbor, an apology for making fun of me about the tree." She picks up another envelope. "This one's from another neighbor, thanking me for being so generous to those in need."

Phil helps Mary gather up the rest of the envelopes. He hands her his stack and walks her to the door. When he bends down and touches his lips to hers, Mary's stomach somersaults and her knees go weak.

"Can I see you tomorrow? I'd like to take you to dinner."

Mary smiles softly. "I'd love that."

He kisses her again, a gentle peck on the cheek, before disappearing down the sidewalk into the dark night.

Mary takes the stack of envelopes upstairs to her room. Changing into her pajamas, she crawls into bed and reads every one of her neighbors' apologies and thank-yous. Even little Tommy writes, saying he's sorry for calling her a grumpy old witch.

Mary dreams that night of brighter days ahead. And when she wakes at dawn the following morning, the ground at the base of the maple tree is bare.

Thank you for reading CAREFUL WHAT YOU WISH, and don't miss any of the books in the Wishing Tree series.

★ Don't miss a Wishing Tree book! ★

Book 1: The Wishing Tree – prologue book
Book 2: I Wish.. by Amanda Prowse
Book 3: Wish You Were Here by Kay Bratt
Book 4: Wish Again by Tammy L. Grace
Book 5: Workout Wishes & Valentine Kisses by Barbara Hinske
Book 6: A Parade of Wishes by Camille Di Maio
Book 7: Careful What You Wish by Ashley Farley
Book 8: Gone Fishing by Jessie Newton
Book 9: Wishful Thinking by Kay Bratt
Book 10: Overdue Wishes by Tammy L. Grace
Book 11: A Whole Heap of Wishes by Amanda Prowse
Book 12: Wishes of Home by Barbara Hinske
Book 13: Wishful Witness by Tonya Kappes

Be sure to check for more books in the Wishing Tree series! We also invite you to join us in our My Book Friends group on Facebook. It's a great place to chat about all things bookish and learn more about our founding authors.

We also invite you to join the authors in our My Book Friends group on Facebook. It's a great place to chat about all things bookish and learn more about our founding authors.

ABOUT THE AUTHOR

Ashley Farley writes books about women for women. Her characters are mothers, daughters, sisters, and wives facing real-life issues. Her bestselling Sweeney Sisters series has touched the lives of many.

Ashley is a wife and mother of two young adult children. While she's lived in Richmond, Virginia, for the past twenty-one years, a piece of her heart remains in the salty marshes of the South Carolina Lowcountry, where she still calls home. Through the eyes of her characters, she captures the moss-draped trees, delectable cuisine, and kindhearted folk with lazy drawls that make the area so unique.

Ashley loves to hear from her readers. Visit Ashley's Website.

Get free exclusive content by signing up for her newsletter.

Facebook
Instagram
Amazon

Made in United States
Orlando, FL
23 February 2024